The Nightmare
and the Unicorn

The Nightmare
and the Unicorn

by

Susan Brown

Yellow Farmhouse Publications

The Nightmare and the Unicorn
Publication Date: 2021
Print edition ISBN: 978-1-950402-03-8

Yellow Farmhouse Publications, Lake Stevens, WA 98258
© Susan Brown 2021

This is a work of fiction. Names, characters, places and incidents are either the product of the author's imagination or are used fictitiously, and any resemblance to actual persons, living or dead, business establishments, events or locales is entirely coincidental.

Excerpt from *Twelve* © 2021 by Susan Brown
Excerpt from *Dragons of Frost and Fire* © 2015 by Susan Brown

Cover Photography: *Teen girl and horse* © Sarah Ros, Shutterstock; *Twilight on a field covered with flowers in summer morning with fog* © Emelianov Evgenii, AdobeStock

For my wonderful daughters, Laurel,
Heather, and Karen who have
helped me, put up with me, and
never stopped cheering me on.

And for the writers who have helped me
with horse facts, ideas, and editing:
Shannon Kennedy, Toni Kief, Linda Jordan,
and the brilliant authors of the Writers
Cooperative of the Pacific Northwest
Thank you!

Books by Susan Brown
www.susanbrownwrites.com

Fantasy:
Twelve

The Nightmare and the Unicorn

Dragons of Earth, Sea, Fire, and Air series:

> Dragons of Frost and Fire
>
> Dragons of Desert and Dust
>
> Dragons of Wind and Waves
>
> A Thunder of Dragons
>
> * New! Boxed Set includes *Dragons of Frost and Fire, Dragons of Desert and Dust, Dragons of Wind and Waves, A Thunder of Dragons* – Find it on Amazon!

The Adventure Books:
Hey, Chicken Man!

Pirates, Prowlers, and Cherry Pie

Sammy and the Devil Dog

Not Yet Summer

The Amber and Elliot Mysteries with Anne Stephenson:
Something's Fishy at Ash Lake

The Mad Hacker

The Secret of Ash Manor

Written with Anne Stephenson as Stephanie Browning:

Outbid by the Star
Undone by the Boss
Making Up is Hard to Do
The Boy She Left Behind, *An All American Boy Romance*

Short Story Collections:

Holiday Cheers: *Stories to Celebrate Your Year*
Romance in Pajama Pants: *Stories to Celebrate Your Happily Ever After*
Romance Sweet and Dark: *The Patchwork of Love*
Last Dance at the Polka Dot Restaurant: *And Other Travels Through Life*
Fantasy Shorts: *Stories to Tickle Your Wonder*

The Nightmare and the Unicorn

Contents

Chapter 1

A flash of lightning and crack of thunder caused Sky to jerk against the car's worn seatbelt. Shaking with exhaustion and repressed anger, she looked over at her mom. Lindey peered anxiously through the sheeting rain, gripping the steering wheel until her knuckles whitened. She glanced at her daughter and forced a smile.

"Almost there..." her voice trailed off. "Can you feel it Sky?" Lindey's voice shook with longing. "Can you feel the magic? The legend says it comes from the horses..."

"All I'm feeling is tired." Sky pushed back the hair that had fallen forward over her face with the last lurch of the car. "We've been on the road for two days. You know what he'll do if he catches us....and you want to talk fairy tales."

"They're not fairy tales," Lindey insisted. "It's real. It happened."

"Yeah. Sure." Sky didn't care. Not when they were running for their lives. Not when she knew what the Nightmare would do if he caught them. Another one of her mother's desperate plans. But this time Sky had insurance against the Nightmare safely tucked in her jacket pocket. Would it be enough? Another flash of lightning and crack of thunder made her wince and press back against the seat.

"I know you think it's crazy," her mom persisted. "But you've got to know why our family has horse magic."

Sky stared out the window – too tired and too terrified to argue with her mother. Maybe if she just let her talk, they could get her back to sense. Back to the reason they had taken this insane journey.

Her mom's voice went singsong from the thousandth repetition. "The Whitmore women have horse magic. It's all because my great-grandmother saved a unicorn."

"Unicorn. Right," Sky muttered. Reluctantly, she felt slightly soothed by the words. This was the story she'd believed in when she was a kid. The one that backed up the big, stupid promise that everything would be okay. The one she had tried so hard to believe. The one that had trapped them.

Lindey's voice rose over the growl of the motor and the roar of wind. "Nearly a hundred years ago, there was this herd of wild horses – beautiful, strong. But the ranchers wanted them slaughtered to free up grazing land for cattle. My great-grandmother was fourteen, just like you, Sky, but she stopped the kill by running into the middle of the herd. And just like a miracle, the horses quieted.

"Then, one by one, the horses stepped back and the unicorn came. It was his herd she'd saved. He touched her with his silver horn. He...he promised..." Her mom's voice shook. "He promised he would come if she needed help." Lindey paused, face shadowed then illuminated as lightning exploded across the night. "No matter how much I needed it, Sky, I never saw a unicorn. But the women in our family are all horsewomen."

"I've never been on a horse," Sky said wearily.

"Yeah, but it's in your blood, and I promise Aunt Judy'll get you on a horse." Her mom looked worriedly down the dark road as their headlights flashed against the white pasture fences and the wall of rain.

Sky leaned forward to stare out too, hoping to get a glimpse of some horses – real ones, not her mom's crazy story about a unicorn galloping in the Pacific Northwest fog. Throughout the endless scramble to pay rent, keep a job, build a life for the two of them, her mom had never stopped talking about the horses. About the yellow farmhouse where she had grown up. About her Aunt Judy who had long ago taught her to train horses. About the home where they would finally be safe from the Nightmare.

Suddenly Lindey cranked the wheel. Sky's shoulder banged against the passenger door as the car abruptly turned into a gravel driveway almost hidden by thick shrubs.

"Those bushes weren't so big before," her mom said apologetically.

Sky rubbed her shoulder and stared at the house. It was just the way her mom had described it – square, butter-yellow, steep red roof over its second story, big and evenly spaced windows on the ground floor, and a wide covered porch at the back. Light shone warmly through uncurtained windows on the lower floor.

Sky leaned toward the light as the car rumbled over the driveway. On either side, pale roses glimmered through the dripping shrubs – more splashes of light against the night. A big yard, shadowed by more shrubs, stretched into the night with a big shed at the end.

The car lurched and stopped. Lindey switched off the ignition and for a moment they sat silently, staring at the farmhouse they had driven so long to reach.

"Remember, Sky," her mom said, "don't say anything about..."

"Not like I'll forget," Sky snapped, "but are you sure? Can you trust her? If Aunt Judy knew what happened...?"

Her mom gripped Sky's arm tightly, fear stiffening her fingers.

"I'm not sure about anything," she whispered. "I ran away and abandoned all this ages ago. But coming back, in spite of my mistakes, is the best chance we have. Don't say anything! Please! Promise me."

"I told you. I've promised." Sky pulled back her arm.

"Well then, let's do it." Her mom shoved open the rusted car door.

Yanking on the broken passenger door's handle until it opened, Sky stepped out, stumbling from cramped muscles and exhaustion. But she didn't make a sound as she swung her backpack over one thin shoulder and marched through the rain up to the covered porch. Carrying her own pack, her mom followed.

"Ready?" Not waiting for her daughter's nod, Lindey rapped on the wood frame. "Hope she's home...."

Sky noticed her mom was breathing hard, short breaths through flared nostrils; she had run her fingers through her hair so often, it had tangled like someone lost in tonight's storm. The bruises on her cheek and jaw shaded to murky green in the porch light. Sky looked away from her mom's tired face and tried to peer through the door's glass panes. A moment later, a light warmed the kitchen and a woman strode forward. A black dog, the size of a small cow, woofed beside her.

"Who's there?" the woman demanded, staring out into the half-light.

"Aunt Judy, it's me – Lindey. Your niece."

"Lindey? *Lindey!*"

The door swung open. A middle-aged woman in jeans and a faded sweatshirt with graying, frizzy hair pulled into a ponytail, gripped the collar of the dog with one hand and held out the other in welcome. The dog strained against her hand, broke loose and galumphed to Sky, plopping on his wiggling rear as he thrust his muzzle into her stomach in greeting.

"He's harmless." Aunt Judy held out her arms and, with a swallowed sob, Sky's mom stepped into the offered hug.

Sky looked straight into the dog's great brown eyes and sank to her knees. The dog laid his mammoth head on her shoulder in welcome, slobbering on her jacket.

"Hello," Sky whispered. Obligingly, the dog snuffled her ear and swashed a great wet tongue over her chin and cheek.

"Moose! Stop that!" Aunt Judy stepped back, keeping one arm around her niece's waist as she spoke to Sky. "He looks like a monster, but I swear he won't hurt you. I have an absolute rule that monsters are never allowed on my property."

"We've made friends." Sky stood and dropped her hand to the shoulder of the panting beast now leaning against her so hard she had to brace her feet to stay upright.

"He's a good judge of character." Aunt Judy's eyes swung back to her niece. "Lindey, you've waited so long. Fourteen years!" She looked hard at Sky. "So, this is your little girl? I thought you were in California, living the dream – cooking for some big hotel?"

Lindey's smile wavered. "I was. But you know what the times are. I got laid off. So here we are."

Aunt Judy peered at her. "That's quite a bruise on your face."

Lindey leaned over to scratch Moose's head. "I tripped and fell – hit my face on a railing."

"Uh huh. And I'm queen of Kalamazoo." Aunt Judy's expression was stern, but she stepped aside and gestured them in. "Come in and sit down. Can I make you a sandwich?" Her attention turned back Sky who was still standing close beside the dog. "And what's your name? I remember it's something unusual. Hippy sounding."

Lindey forced a laugh. "Even you are way too young for the hippy generation, Aunt Judy. Her name's Skylark...but she goes by Sky."

"And how old are you, Sky?"

"Fourteen," Lindey said, "but she's mature for her age."

Aunt Judy looked over the straight, thin girl before her. "You don't look fourteen."

With a nearly suppressed jab of irritation, Sky met her eyes steadily. "How old are you?"

"Fifty-three."

"You look fifty-three. One day you'll probably look sixty-three, but it won't change when you were born."

"Sky!" Lindey interrupted, pulling her daughter close.

Aunt Judy's cool grey eyes met the steely blue ones. "No, I guess it won't. Do you always say what you think?"

Sky twisted away from her mom and stood straight again.

"I'm sorry, Aunt Judy." Lindey grimaced and turned to her aunt. "We've driven all the way from California without hardly stopping. Can we sit down a bit?"

"Of course." With a slightly lurching step, Aunt Judy led them toward a living room that was furnished simply with a blanket-covered recliner, coffee table, and sofa, and cluttered with bookshelves, framed art, and overgrown plants. A big TV droned on one wall. Aunt Judy motioned them to the blue and brown, striped sofa, moved a pile of books from the cushions to the coffee table, and switched off the set.

"Get comfortable," Aunt Judy said. "So Lindey, after hardly a word in years, why are you here?"

Sky watched as her mom smiled her best smile and relaxed her shoulders. But she twisted her fingers and her skin flushed against the smudgy circles under her eyes.

"Aunt Judy," she began, "I'm desperate. I...we need a place to stay for a few days. My money's gone, but I've got a job – a good job – lined up...I just won't get paid for a week or two. And...I can't take Sky to a shelter or leave her in the car. Please...will you help us?"

Sky's eyes widened a bit at the lie. She and her mom had been in shelters before and slept in the car a couple of times too. But the Nightmare had always found them and made them come back. Sky felt her own fingers curling into fists. Her Mom had told her that this time they would keep going until they got away from him – that they would never go back to the Nightmare's world again. That he wouldn't be able to trace the old wreck of a car she'd bought. That they could live in the safety of the yellow farmhouse. But starting with a string of lies seemed like a stupid idea.

"Explain," Judy said.

"Sky, do you need to go to the bathroom or anything?" Lindey prompted.

Reluctantly recognizing her mom's cue, Sky nodded and stood up. Aunt Judy pointed to the hallway and said, "At the end."

Sky went, made noise closing the door, and slipped back to the edge of the hallway. Her heart was pounding but she kept her breath soft. Since the Nightmare had stolen their lives, she'd made it a rule to always listen.

"There isn't much to explain," Lindey murmured. "You know what it's like trying to get a job these days. I jumped at the chance of this one in Seattle. Closer to home. But I don't have any money, so I'm hoping that you would help us out for a few days."

"What about the money you inherited from your mother?" Aunt Judy's voice was razor sharp. Sky could picture her mom smiling the right smile, and then dropping her eyes. Even now, after everything, her mom wasn't much of a liar. Sky willed her mom to get it right. They didn't have anywhere else to go. She'd promised they would be safe. That Aunt Judy could protect them – even from the Nightmare. Sky no longer trusted that anyone could protect them. Her fingers slid over the lump in her pocket, reassuring herself that her insurance was still there. Fiercely, she told herself again that nothing could drag her back. Nothing.

"This isn't the first time I've been out of work...and a child costs a lot. Maybe I made some bad decisions."

That's for sure, Sky thought.

"Drugs?" Aunt Judy demanded.

"No!" Lindey's voice was vehement. "Never. I hate drugs. I know what they do."

There was silence. Sky eased back to the bathroom and flushed the toilet. She turned on the tap and then slid back to her listening post.

"I won't give you money," Aunt Judy said.

"And I didn't ask for any," Lindey retorted. "But Aunt Judy...I could use a place for us to stay for a few days. And you're the only family we've got." Sky heard the catch in her mom's voice. "I wanted Sky to see where I grew up, the place I loved before I made all those dumb mistakes...." Her voice trailed off but there was no answering sound from Aunt Judy. "Does...is Neil McClelland still raising thoroughbreds?"

"Yes," Aunt Judy said. "Winners, too." She paused. "His breeding and training programs are flawless," she said grudgingly. "His horses are some of the best in the country and they've made him rich. Are you thinking you can whisper his horses again? After everything?"

Silence. Bitterly, Sky pictured her mom's bowed head, her helpless tears.

Judy spoke again, but her voice suddenly sounded troubled. "He's got a new horse...a beautiful creature. But utterly, completely wild. Neil can't do a thing with him." Sky had to strain now to hear her aunt's voice. "There's something about that stallion that's calling for horse magic, Lindey. Did you lose your magic when you ran away from here? Have you...can you?"

Sky pressed closer to the wall. A thrill, unexpected and intense, caught her breath. She tried to push it away, but her childhood dreams had always been about horses, about the beautiful creatures her mom said she'd loved and trained. In the darkest of times, Sky imagined herself riding bareback through flower-laden fields or standing perfectly balanced, arms outspread, her body swaying easily to the perfect rhythm of a perfect horse. Free...

Lindey's sob broke open Sky's dreams. "No..." her mom said. "My gift is gone. I looked for a job at a stable in LA but the horses can't hear me any more. You were right, Aunt Judy. When I ran away, my magic died."

"I'm sorrier than I can say," Aunt Judy said softly.

"But I can still muck out a stable." There was a thin edge of longing in her mom's voice.

"I don't keep horses any more," Aunt Judy said bluntly. "Six years ago, I took a bad fall, broke my leg and hip." Silence stretched out. "You know Neil won't welcome you."

Sky heard her mother's weary assent.

"I've never met anyone who could make as many mistakes as you, Lindey," Aunt Judy said. "But I still see the goodness in you. The two of you can stay."

"Thanks...thanks, Aunt Judy."

So relieved she had to force back tears, Sky went back into the bathroom, turned off the tap, and returned to the living room. Her mom was leaning back into the sofa cushions in exhaustion, but her face twitched into a small smile. "Hey kiddo," she said, pulling her into a hug as though she were four, not fourteen. "How about we stay here for a few days?"

Resting her head against her mom's shoulder for a moment, Sky looked at Aunt Judy, assessing. Aunt Judy returned the gaze, also assessing. *She isn't sure she likes us...me...*

Sky realized. She gave an inward shrug. *We'll fix our lives without the old woman's help.*

Somehow.

Moose huffed and collapsed into a pile at her feet, his head resting on her knees. Sky dug her fingers into his soft fur and suddenly felt her eyes droop in the exhaustion she couldn't fight off any longer. Later, after she had chewed through half a sandwich and gulped a mug of hot sweet tea, she stumbled after Aunt Judy upstairs to a small bedroom. Stripped to her underwear, Sky crawled under a pink flowered quilt, letting her hand trail over the side to rest on Moose's massive head. *Sleep... finally sleep....*

*   *   *

The next morning, the sun was barely up when a noise woke Sky. Completely still in the unfamiliar room, Sky searched her memory for where she was. *Aunt Judy's house.* A second sharp bang. Sky yanked herself out of bed, and, hands pressed against the glass, watched through the window. Below, her mom's car choked and revved. Sky tried to slow her breathing as the memories flooded her mind.

The plan. *The plan to escape the Nightmare.* Sky shivered. He must not find them again.

Never. Bitterly, she remembered her mom's statements that Aunt Judy's "magic" was enough to ward off the Nightmare's horror. How could her mother believe in fairy tales after what they'd suffered?

When the car turned onto the road and grumbled away out of sight, Sky got back into bed and pulled the quilt up over her head. She made her breath stop coming in harsh gasps, until eventually she drifted back to sleep.

Her old dream came again. She rode a white horse, standing, arms outstretched, rising and falling, light as a moonbeam in the rhythm of pounding hooves and glistening magic.

Susan Brown

Chapter 2

The alarm buzzed Jeremy awake, drilling through a brilliant dream of snowboarding down the mountain pass. He groaned softly, slapped the snooze button and collapsed onto his pillow. No use. Sleep was gone. Shoving his hair out of his eyes, he looked over to see the dawn light stealing through his window, shining a rainbow in the long crack he'd made years ago with a wildly thrown baseball. Jeremy's lips twitched into a ghost of a smile – that was the last time his older brother had tried to move him toward the coolness of team sports jockdom. Mike had known a lost cause when he saw it.

With a grunt, Jeremy heaved himself out of bed and, after a stop in the bathroom, pulled on old jeans, a torn sweatshirt, and stained sneakers. He passed into the kitchen, turning his eyes away from the sight of his dad asleep and snoring in the living room recliner. There was an odor of stale beer lying heavily in the room.

In the kitchen, Jeremy slipped an apple into his pocket and took out the carton of milk. He drank quickly, gulping so fast he almost choked. Then wiping his sleeve across his mouth, he put the milk back on the shelf. His mom had gotten mad when he or Mike drank from the milk carton, but she wouldn't have much liked his dad getting drunk all alone at night either.

For a moment, Jeremy felt a rush of guilt and a horde of other putrid emotions – his mom would hate the way the family was all wrong. Mike had gone away to college, Jeremy practically sleepwalked through his days, and his dad...Jeremy's mouth formed a thin line... all day his dad did the right things – went to work, bought groceries, made sure Jeremy had clean clothes and Mike had money for tuition. But at night that fragile mask disappeared and his dad got lost in beer. No one in the family laughed any more. All the happiness and fun had been cremated with his mom last fall.

But just like every day, even on the day of the funeral, the horses still had to be fed. Moving silently, so as not to wake his father, Jeremy went out the kitchen door and, hands in his pockets and breath puffing vapor, trudged out to the barn. He turned their six horses out into the field, but depending on their horsey personalities, they trotted or walked or galloped back toward him as he forked sweet hay into the wheelbarrow. Like he always did, Jeremy called out to each one while he worked.

"Hey Molly, you need to tell that colt of yours not to run so hard up to the fence. Hear that, Rook? If you're going too fast, you'll slam into it. Then Mr. McClelland won't want you for his stable. You want to be a champion, don't you?" He turned to the big stallion watching from the second pasture. "What about you, Prince Caspian? Maybe you can give your son some pointers." The old horse eyed him with dignity, but then snorted. Jeremy laughed. "He's not that bad. Just young. Look at Fledge. Two years ago she was a crazy filly and now she's learning everything we can teach her. Pretty soon she'll be a high-stepper – as good at dressage as Molly or Firefly. Just you wait."

Jeremy pitched the hay over the fence into several piles. Once that was done, he checked that the troughs were full of clean water and put away the fork and wheelbarrow. Blowing on his hands, he watched the horses for a while, listening to them huffing and snorting as they lipped up the hay. He wondered if he should ride Molly today, put her through her paces. Molly had been his mom's horse – they had won a lot of competitions together. Dad had said they ought to sell her, being so valuable and all, but not one of them could face sending her off to a new owner.

So instead, Dad had made a deal with Mr. McClelland to breed her with Prince Caspian. The showy black horse had never been a big winner in the circuit or Neil McClelland wouldn't have agreed. Their neighbor was notorious for his hard bargains so it was no surprise to Jeremy that Neil had insisted that they look after Prince Caspian and then he would take first rights on the foal. Jeremy hoped Rook was too small for national competitions. The colt was the only good thing that had happened to the family in more than two years and he wanted to train Rook himself. Neil was good to his horses, but Jeremy's mom had been one of the Whitmores. She'd taught him some of her horse magic – the secret of whispering his thoughts to the beautiful animals.

Jeremy clucked his tongue and Molly, head bobbing, walked over to the fence. For a moment, he rubbed the insides of her ears with his thumbs, loving the sound of her blowing questions and stamping hooves. She knew there was an apple waiting in his pocket.

"Do you miss her?" Jeremy asked. "Do you remember Mom?"

Molly tossed her head. Jeremy accepted that as a yes and offered her the apple. She took it delicately, fastening her big teeth on the fruit and wiggling her soft lips to hold the apple while she crunched contentedly. Jeremy gave her one last pat and turned toward the house. Just then, a loud bang – a car backfiring – echoed across the field. Two of the horses snorted in panic.

Volcanic anger, erupting from somewhere deep inside, made Jeremy start spitting swears. An old car turned out of Judy Whitmore's driveway, backfired again like a gunshot, and roared away down the road. His eyes caught the flicker of a curtain in an upstairs bedroom, but the shrill neighs of the horses yanked his attention away from any curiosity he might have had. Firefly and Fledge were shaking, tossing their heads and half-prancing, eyes wide at the frightening noise. Speaking softly, calling sweetness to them, Jeremy climbed over the fence and spent the next few minutes reassuring the two skittery mares. As they calmed from the unexpected noise, nuzzling his neck and lipping his hair, the startling fury subsided.

When the horses were quiet and his hands about frozen in the cold morning air, Jeremy headed back into the house. He sniffed appreciatively at the smell of coffee.

"Horses okay?" his dad asked, squinting a little at the light that flashed through the opened door.

"Yeah, a car spooked them, but they settled down." Jeremy pushed the door shut as gently as he could and sat at the kitchen table. "Looks like it might come on to rain again later, so I was thinking of working with Molly after breakfast."

"Mmm," his dad answered. "Want some coffee?"

"Sure."

His dad poured out two mugs and took the carton of milk from the fridge. Jeremy filled his mug to the brim with milk and wrapped his cold hands around it.

"Dad?" He hesitated.

His dad grunted and sat opposite, nursing his own drink.

"Dad?" Jeremy started again.

"What?" His dad's eyes were swollen and red, half-open. The stubble on his chin and cheeks gave him a muzzy, undefined look.

"Do you think you should be drinking so much?" Jeremy's heart pounded but he tried to keep his face passive. It wasn't working. He could feel his anger flaring again.

"I think you should mind your own business." His father's voice was hard, like a stranger's. "You're not wanting for anything. And I don't know where you think you got a right to talk to me like that. Maybe you should worry instead about getting your math grades up past a D."

"That...the math...that has nothing to do with it!" Jeremy stammered. "It has nothing to do with you drinking every night."

His dad seemed to try to become reasonable, to ignore the anger seething between them. "I look after my business, Jeremy. You look after yours."

The volcano inside him was erupting again. Jeremy thrust himself away from the table. As he flung out the door, he shot over his shoulder, "It didn't just happen to you, Dad. Mom dying didn't just happen to you."

Was there anything in the universe that could turn right all the wrongness in their lives these days? Jeremy nearly ran back to the horses, reaching out to them for their warmth and comfort.

*   *   *

Sky dressed slowly, pulling on her last clean shirt, and a sweatshirt over it. There was a two-day-old ketchup smudge on her jeans. Moose nudged her with his head and tentatively licked the spot. She felt an unaccustomed giggle bubble up – that was twice she'd laughed since she got here. Maybe there was some kind of magic in this house after all. Yeah, right. Sky straightened up and decided that even if her heart was bungee jumping in her chest, she had better scope everything out right now.

Cautiously, she pushed her door open. The second floor of Aunt Judy's house seemed small. The stairs joined the hallway almost in front of Sky's room; the bathroom lay opposite a few steps away, and another short corridor led to a room that was out of Sky's line of vision. A sound of clicking computer keys was faintly audible. Sky rubbed her hands on her thighs, trying to decide what her first move should be.

The bathroom. Definitely the bathroom.

A few moments later, Sky lingered in the hallway again, still listening to the *tip tap* of keys, wondering if she should interrupt, return to her bedroom, or venture downstairs. Moose, obviously bored with her indecision, woofed imperiously. The typing stopped and Aunt Judy called out. "Moose! I hope you didn't wake up that girl!"

"No, I'm awake," Sky said. She didn't like being called *that girl*, but she pasted a smile on her face and stepped into the other room. It had been set up as a weird kind of office – computers, printers, and stacks of paper were arranged with precision along a wall-length table. Everywhere else, plants wove upwards along window sashes, rested against rock crystals, and even twined across the bookshelves that lined the room. The shelves were piled high and many of the volumes had paper markers sticking out of them. Framed photos of horses and a younger Aunt Judy, and a girl...maybe her mother...holding up winners' ribbons covered the rest of the wall space.

Aunt Judy swung around on a swivel chair, away from the computer. She wore the same type of jeans and sweatshirt as she had last night, although in a different color. Her hair was no longer in a ponytail but stuck out in a crinkly halo around her head.

"Good morning," Aunt Judy said. "I have a terrifyingly tight deadline for my new book about horse training. I haven't heard your mom yet, but there's milk and juice in the fridge and I left cereal and English muffins on the counter. Bowls and glasses are in the cupboard. Just search until you find whatever you need...what's your name again? Sky! Help yourself to whatever you want, Sky. And tell your mom to go ahead and make coffee or tea whenever she gets up. The two of you looked done in last night. Okay, I've got to get back to work. I swear these deadlines are going to kill me...."

She swiveled back to her computer and the rapid *tip tap* began again. Above her head, a prism hung in the window with sunlight streaming through it, creating rainbow fragments that drifted serenely across the walls.

Sky left the doorway and silently made her way downstairs. Unbidden, a four-year-old memory flashed across her mind.

"The kid's a spook," the Nightmare had growled when he had not heard her enter the kitchen.

"I'm sorry." Like a servant, her mom held the plate of toast out to him.

The Nightmare scowled and threw a piece of toast on the floor. "Want breakfast, Spook?" he taunted. "There! Help yourself."

Sky retreated – she knew better than to turn her back on him. She was screaming inside for that bread, but she wouldn't let the Nightmare see her scramble for it. Never, ever. Even if she did starve.

For a moment Sky breathed hard, like she'd been running, but then she tightened her lips and went into the kitchen. The food was laid out, just as Aunt Judy had said, and a kettle sat ready on the stove with a tea canister and an oversized sugar bowl beside it. Sky longed for more sweet tea, but didn't want the kettle's whistle to attract her great-aunt's attention.

Refusing to let the memory rush her, Sky made herself a large breakfast of a buttered English muffin with home-made raspberry jam followed by a brimming bowl of cereal with milk. She ate standing, chewing rapidly, silently, eyes darting around the kitchen. More rock crystals gleamed on the windowsill, their geometric forms throwing patterns of fractured light across the walls. Even more plants leaned vigorously toward the streaming sunlight. The room felt awake and alive.

Sky frowned. The Nightmare's perfectly furnished house had felt dead and she had felt nearly dead living in it. Shaking her head, Sky felt a surge of hope. But she'd been beaten down so often that she pushed the hope aside too. It could be as much of a trap as those cruel games the Nightmare played.

Despite the thrust of growing things, the dancing sunlight, and her mom's repeated promise that Aunt Judy's mojo magic would protect them, Sky knew this plan relied way too much on her mom's hopeful fantasies. That old woman hadn't even realized her niece had left.

How can she keep out monsters, Sky thought scornfully. *She doesn't even know what's happening in her own house.*

Blinking back angry tears, Sky dropped her hand to caress Moose's soft ears. A nice house with a nice dog was a stupid reason to stop being smart. Her mom had gone. Aunt Judy was just an old woman. Sky had to depend on herself, and food was the first thing. Ever since the Nightmare had...Sky shook her head to block the memory. She just had to make sure there would be food.

Laying her partially eaten muffin on the counter, Sky took another, thickly buttering and spreading it with jam. Quietly hunting through the cupboards, she found a sandwich bag, eased it out of the box so the package didn't look disturbed, and then sealed the second muffin within the plastic. She would need a handy hiding place where her food stash could be quickly retrieved in an emergency.

Not even her mom had guessed how good she was at survival.

Moose stared at her and then glanced meaningfully at the muffin, drool seeping from his mouth. He pointedly ignored a big dish filled with dried dog food a few feet away. Sky muffled another laugh and gave him the crust of her unfinished muffin. How could she resist those eyes?

Then, moving silently again, Sky returned to her small bedroom. A tall bookcase crammed with books took up one wall.

Tip, tap came steadily from Aunt Judy's office.

Reaching up, Sky slid the bagged sandwich behind the volumes on the top shelf. Then she took the flash drive from her sweatshirt pocket, and carefully wedged it between books on the bottom shelf. For a moment she stood, irresolute. It was such a tiny shield against the Nightmare – but it was all she had.

Unsure now what her next move should be, Sky went to the window. Across the road, a teenage boy was riding a gleaming brown horse. To Sky's startled eyes, it appeared that the horse almost danced under the boy's sure hands and shifting body.

She couldn't resist. Drawn as if by magic, Sky ran silently downstairs and out the kitchen door, Moose at her heels.

Breathing hard, heart soaring, Sky and Moose raced across the road, stopping at the white board fence. She climbed up the bottom rail and leaned forward as if the whinnies and snorts of the horses summoned her.

The brown horse danced in the early spring grass, the sun shone warmly, and the thought flashed across Sky's mind, that despite everything, maybe she had found true magic – a home.

Chapter 3

"Homework!" Athena's mom announced, finger uplifted as though inspiration had texted down from the heavens. "I know you must have homework!"

"Not on the first morning of spring break," Athena replied brightly. Grabbing her camera, she went out the front door, letting it slam behind her.

With her *Portraits of the Famous* photographic show now open in New York, Ellen Faviola had returned home and was on a new "devoted mother" crusade. Athena sighed. Would she survive being so thoroughly parented? Her mom had trouble remembering she was sixteen not six, and there were at least five weeks to get through before her mother's next contract distracted her.

How would Athena and her dad survive it?

Whenever her mother traipsed around the world on one of her big assignments, Athena and her dad happily went about their days, Athena taking digital photos and fitting high school in when she must, and her dad building fine wood furniture and fitting his construction job in when he must. Sometimes Athena wondered if she and her laid-back dad were her globe-trotting mom's anchors, or if they dragged her down.

Zipping her jacket against the chill of a gusty wind, Athena strolled along the verge of the road, eyes searching for likely subjects. She'd shot and made digital magic with the bank of cedars by the Whitmore place so many times she was sick of them.

Horses, maybe? If she could get Jeremy Stolz to pose, that would be something, but she doubted whether he'd cooperate. Most of the kids at school saw him as this over-sized, round-faced kid who needed a haircut and kept his mouth shut; but Athena had seen him reach out his big hands and soft voice to those terrifyingly huge horses. Each and every one dropped its head and nuzzled him like an adoring puppy. It was magic. No other explanation. And as an artist, Athena had tried really, really hard to catch that sorcery with her camera. So far, she had not been able to capture even a ghost of Jeremy's gifts.

A bug flew up from the grass and landed on Athena's glasses. She blew a sharp puff of air upwards, dislodging a strand of hair so that it flopped, dark and curly over her face and into her mouth. The bug still crawled over her glasses.

"Phooey," she spat out the hair, pulled off her glasses and shook the bug loose. It buzzed happily away.

"I hate the country," she announced to her surroundings. As usual, there was no answer.

Stomping along the road towards Stolz's fields, she tripped over a discarded drink can. "Littering cretins," she muttered and shoved her glasses back up the bridge of her nose. Later, if it wasn't raining, she'd come out with a garbage bag and clear the detritus that had accumulated since her last save-the-earth efforts.

Pushing her way around an overgrown camellia bush that waved ruffly pink flowers right into the road, Athena stopped at the edge of the pasture.

"*Aha!*" She had struck it rich! Jeremy was riding that beautiful brown mare. To Athena's enraptured eyes, they looked like a dance couple. Her fingers flew to adjust angles and settings, rapidly netting the performance frame after frame. Too soon, Jeremy turned his horse toward the barn.

"*Ah...ratatouille!*" Athena flicked back through the shots, not entirely pleased with any. Maybe some computer work later would improve them. The deadline for the online photo contest was midnight tonight and despite days and days of work, she didn't have anything special to submit.

Discontentedly, she scanned the field for more subjects. An unfamiliar girl leaned over the fence, slim body bending toward the horses like a compass needle turned north. Judy Whitmore's big dog, Moose, panted in the grass beside her.

Athena stared for a moment, assessing the possibilities of approaching this girl.

Minus – the girl looked painfully younger than her own sixteen years (*ergo*, she probably would not have anything interesting to say or be able to pose seriously for a picture).

Plus – there were no other kids for miles (other than terminally shy Jeremy).

Minus – the really big minus – there was that humungous canine that would probably leap on her and then, with waterfalls of drool dripping onto her doomed body, chew off each of her legs and then slowly devour the rest of her with great crunching, doggy joy.

Athena was very aware that her short and stocky (but not fat) build would topple like a stack of blocks if that monster attacked. Not worth it. Definitely not worth it.

Decision made, Athena faded back behind the camellia before the girl or dog spotted her.

Maybe there would be some trilliums open in the woods behind Judy Whitmore's house, or even something interesting happening at McClelland's stables. If she hadn't put off driving classes, Athena thought glumly, she could have gone somewhere more attention-grabbing. But cars were almost as terrifying as big animals.

"Self-selected limitations," she accused herself. Still muttering frustration, she crossed the road and slid through a gap in the fence where ancient plum trees had slowly pushed apart the wire. Slipping behind the trees, she waded through the undergrowth that formed an acre-wide swath of brush separating the two properties.

Dark and wild, just like Judy Whitmore and Neil McClelland, her mom had said. Those two had encouraged that wilderness to grow up between them. "Judy Whitmore is…eccentric," her mom had said. "And Neil is about as flexible as a fence post. They've been bringing out the worst in each other for years!"

Athena's phone shrilled. She pulled it from her pocket and checked the display – *Mom*. Smiling, Athena silenced the ringer. "Call away, mother," she said. "I am so unavailable."

She crouched by a wildflower (or maybe it was a weed) with a stringy stalk and a golden flower, and shot a few pictures, making sure she caught the image of the disturbingly camouflaged spider hiding beneath the petals – pale yellow, blending perfectly into the flower. Athena had seen them before – arachnid hunters dressed to kill in buttery yellow, pure white, and even occasionally white with a pink stripe, all to better blend into flower petals as they waited for prey. Their cunning chilled her.

She glanced up at the sky. A storm was brewing and the rising wind was cold. If she was smart, she'd take off for home, but this weather might make for amazing pictures. Athena licked her lips – lightning. Horses with manes streaming in the wind. Drama.

Her stomach growled noticeably, but the lure of an incredible series of photos was stronger. The trees in Judy's woods would probably be enough shelter. And afterwards, wet but triumphant, her mother might use some of that parenting fervor to whip up a really great lunch. A girl could hope.

Athena fiddled with her camera settings, relishing the rising wind as the storm approached. This was going to be amazing.

*   *   *

It felt good – no, great – to have Molly's graceful, muscled body under him. Jeremy leaned and Molly responded. He twitched the rein and Molly danced sideways, criss-crossing her legs in a playful skip. She tossed her head, clearly enjoying the performance of her skills as much as he did. Jeremy resolved to get back into the routine of riding and training the horses every day, the way he used to do with his mom. It wasn't fair to them to be left so alone – although he had to admit that maybe the horses liked being fat and lazy.

Today he'd have to cut the session short. Clouds were banking on the horizon and the erratic breeze told him a storm, probably a big one, would break before too long. He'd have to get Molly taken care of and the other horses into the barn.

As he directed Molly into a last canter around the pasture, he caught sight of a blonde kid leaning over the fence with Moose flopped on the grass beside her. Jeremy nodded at her, more for the sake of Moose, whom he liked a lot, than anything else. He didn't remember ever seeing the girl before and didn't care much either.

"Hey," the girl called.

Jeremy turned Molly toward the barn, pretending he didn't hear her. His life was complicated enough already. And even if it wasn't that complicated, he just didn't care about anything anymore. Except his horses.

He glanced at the clouds again. They were coming in fast, and they looked like they'd carry thunder and lightning. He had to get his horses into shelter.

*   *   *

Entranced by the sight of the mare, Sky called out to the rider, but he ignored her and disappeared into the barn. Leaning against the fence, she wondered if there was a way to coax a horse over to her. She wished she had an apple or carrot. For a moment she thought about pulling up tufts of long grass, but that seemed pointless when she looked across the big green pasture. True, the horses had cropped the grass short, but it was still grass.

Her mom had said that you didn't need treats for real horse magic – you needed to call them to you in their own language. Right. And she spoke such fluent horse. Just another one of her mom's crazy fantasies. For long moments Sky stared over the fence at the horses, longing to reach out to them. She hadn't had a human friend since the Nightmare came into their lives. The loneliness she'd always determinedly pushed back erupted, tightening her throat. What if she could somehow communicate with these beautiful creatures?

The young horse whinnied and almost instinctively, Sky closed her eyes and, with all other thoughts emptied from her mind, softly called to the horses, mentally asked them to accept her. She pictured them moving over to her, their heads tossing and feet prancing. Even though it felt as if she was reaching through a fog, Sky beckoned them with all her heart.

She opened her eyes when she heard a soft whicker. The colt stood only a few yards away. Was it possible? Could it be happening?

"Friends?" Sky whispered, holding out both hands.

The horse gazed at her then, step by step, moved closer, his head bobbing with each footfall as he searched her face and body for signs that she was safe. Sky held perfectly still, hands outstretched. The black colt brushed and bumped his soft lips over her fingers, the semblance of a kiss as he searched first one hand and then the other for some kind of treat. Heart pounding, Sky held absolutely motionless. Behind the colt, the other horses ambled in her direction, stopping every few feet to twitch their elegant tails, flick their ears, or crop a mouthful of grass, moving in wide zig-zags that brought them closer to her, but cautiously, with their hooves poised to gallop away.

"I'm so glad to meet you," Sky whispered.

One by one, their soft noses nudged her hands and arms as she breathed in their thick, horsey scents and gazed into their wide eyes, all fringed with ridiculously long lashes. Their heads tossed and turned to better look at this new person. Heart pounding, breath catching, as the velvety lips brushed her skin and hands, Sky reached out, fingers trailing across their cheeks and necks.

Magic! For this moment, magic had kissed her thoughts.

For the first time, Sky felt a stirring of hope. Maybe here the Nightmare could be forgotten. Maybe...

*   *   *

Jeremy, having finished unsaddling and grooming Molly, came out of the barn and stopped. His horses, all his horses, were clustered around that skinny girl. Even Prince Caspian, lord of his own pasture, was leaning against the fence, head pivoted toward her. What was she doing? What was she doing to his horses?

"Hey!" he shouted. *"Hey! Get away from there!"*

The angry edge on his voice startled the animals, breaking the connection Sky had forged. One by one they ambled away, forgetting everything except the endless search for tender grass.

The magic shattered. Sky froze just a second and then took to her heels, dashing across the road and weaving through the trees and shrubs until she was sure he would not know where she was. Safe. Maybe safe. Unless the shouter followed Moose's crashing path. She didn't know him. Didn't know if he was just a guy or if he relished pain like the Nightmare had. Trembling, breathing hard, she threw her arm around the dog's thick neck, ignored a sloppy kiss on her cheek, and peered back through the curtain of leaves.

The teen had raced over to the horses and, one by one, was talking to them, rubbing their long noses and soft ears, combing his fingers through their manes and patting their muscled shoulders. They nuzzled him affectionately and then curved their heads down to tear and munch on the grass.

Sky watched as he touched one after another, checking them, connecting with the horses the way she had wanted to. The rising wind ruffled their manes and tails, as one by one he urged them toward the barn. When he did not even glance across the road towards her hiding place, her fear slowly subsided.

Her mom had told her about the intricacies of training, of the people who were horsemen and horsewomen. Maybe this grouchy teenager had magic running through his fingers. The horses seemed to obey him instinctively.

Would she be holed up in the yellow farmhouse for long enough to learn the secrets of horsemanship? Sky knew suddenly that she hungered for that knowledge, the way the Nightmare had made her hungry for food. Not everyone was like the Nightmare, she told herself. But no stupid risks – she had to be careful, very careful. Yet her heart longed for those horses. Sky sank down and began to make plans, spinning pictures of herself astride the horses, feeling their strength and beauty – the safety of freedom and trust.

For a moment, Sky let herself dream – let herself reach for just a tiny wisp of that magic her mother had told her about. Would the unicorn magic of the family legends reach even to her?

The door to the yellow farmhouse opened and Aunt Judy frowned angrily outward. Sky shrank back into the bushes and the dream tendril withered away.

"Stupid," she muttered. No magic for her – just survival. Survival was what really mattered. Daydreams would make her careless. And carelessness could destroy her.

Chapter 4

"Moose! *Moose!*" Aunt Judy's sharp voice shot across the yard. At the sound of his mistress' summons, Moose pricked up his ears, and with a joyful "*Woof!*" bounded out of the shrubs, away from Sky.

She could hear him "*Woof!*" again, like a child shouting, "I'm here! I'm here! Why did you get lost?"

"Moose, you naughty boy," Aunt Judy scolded from the porch. "How did you get out? Did that girl leave the door open?" There was a pause. Through the leaves, Sky watched as Aunt Judy stared at the empty driveway, her face gathering into a frown.

"I don't believe it," she said flatly. "Lindey's gone again. You'd think she would have at least said goodbye. Well, good riddance. Right, Moose?" With that, Aunt Judy and the dog went into the house and closed the door.

Sky sat back on her heels, unconsciously wrapping her arms around her middle for protection. Aunt Judy thought she had driven away with her mother. Why hadn't she said something, right after breakfast? Made some kind of noise to alert her great-aunt that she was still in the house? Stupid again.

Now the door was shut and locked and Sky was out here with no food and nowhere to go. Too quickly, she began to tremble. The months of deprivation and fear had weakened her horribly. One night of sleep and food would not be enough to recover. Sky scrubbed her face, willing herself to pull herself together. The Nightmare thought thin was attractive, so he made sure Sky and her mom stayed thin. For Sky, skinny was another sign of the misery she and her mom had experienced at his hands. But even now, locked out and cold, she wouldn't give in.

What if she just knocked on the door and said, "*I'm back!*" Sky's face heated with humiliation.

Her great-aunt had said, "Good riddance."

A cold, wet drop plopped on her arm. Then another, and another, and another. Sky looked up at the grey clouds, swirling above like dirty cotton candy, thicker and thicker even as she watched. The rain came down harder and harder.

Shelter.

Somewhere she had to find shelter. The Nightmare had locked her out in the rain once and she had been sick for days afterward. She wouldn't waste time or humiliation begging her great-aunt to let her in. There were other buildings...there had to be somewhere to take refuge...the shed at the back of the big lawn. Sky left the bushes, ran through sheeting rain, and yanked at the shed's door.

Locked.

The rain poured down, soaking through her clothes, drenching her hair. The wind rose. Above, thunder rumbled and cracked. A few fields away, lightning speared the ground. Even the huge, old trees around the property swept and bowed, dancing wildly in the gusts. Thunder shattered the air again as the rain lashed down.

Sky wrapped her arms around her body and leaned against the sparse shelter of the shed's wall, fighting to hold back the shivers that ravaged her bony frame too quickly. But she was still flexible and her muscles were strong. Really strong. The Nightmare had paid for those expensive gymnastics lessons because the parents of the other students were mostly wealthy. The Nightmare was a hunter, rich people were his prey, and sometimes Sky was the bait.

A few hailstones thrummed against the wall and then another wave of rain bucketed over her. Sky shivered uncontrollably.

And then, a piercing cry.

Sky's head snapped up. The wind carried the sound of a horse's whinny and then a searing, fear-laden scream. It was a horse. A horse wild with terror.

Thunder exploded and lightning crackled down beyond the far back of Aunt Judy's property. Sky twisted to peer through the rain, past the thick woods. That must be where the stables lay. With sudden hope, Sky straightened. Over there, somewhere, lay the stables with mounds of thick, dry hay, and the warmth of those glorious animals – if she could find it. The vision shot her with new energy. Sky plunged back into the rain and wind, jogging determinedly in the direction of the horse's cry.

But why had a horse cried out in such fear? She had to find it. Had to protect it from its Nightmare.

The woods loomed ahead, edges laced with blackberries and low-growing shrubs. Sky hesitated, now shaking so hard with cold that her head felt thick. What if she couldn't find the horse or the barns? She looked back toward the yellowish blur of the farmhouse. Could she risk Aunt Judy's anger?

Again, the gusts of wind carried the panicked neighs of horses. Sky's head whipped back in the direction of the fields beyond the snarled bramble. She sucked in a ragged breath and kept going.

The thicket rose in front of her. The rain was coming down harder now, sheeting over her face so that she had to push her streaming hair back from her eyes. The wind gusted around her, tossing up the undersides of the leaves. Inch-thick, spiked vines twisted upward into the trees, weaving a thorny barrier.

Desperate, Sky ran back and forth in front of the wall of thorns, looking for a way through. Nothing. Maybe she should go back. But the fear of Aunt Judy telling her that she was useless and not wanted, just like the Nightmare had, oozed across her mind. Sky again scrubbed her face with her hands and tried to wipe away her fear.

A horse screamed.

Thunder rolled across the sky. Lightning cracked.

Gritting her teeth, Sky plunged into the thicket, crying out as thorns tore her skin. She stomped down trying to crush the vines to the ground, but even as big ones bent down, smaller canes sprang upward, whipping through the air, snagging her clothes, catching her hair and raking across her skin. She cried out in pain. Wheals of blood opened on her face and arms.

Twisting, she tried to escape, but the down-curving thorns jabbed and held like fishhooks. Icy water poured from the skies and dripping leaves. Sky shook uncontrollably, but she wouldn't give up. She never gave up. No matter how bad the Nightmare had made it, she never gave up. The brambles knotted themselves behind her. How far forward? How much farther?

More thunder exploded above. A flash of lightning. Branches caught her clothes and hair. Sky screamed, struggling...struggling against the Nightmare...he had grabbed her. Was cutting her. She shouted, twisted and... and broke free, into the safety of the trees.

Safe.

She staggered a few more feet and collapsed, shoulder supported by rough bark, panting, mind spinning. Beneath her, years of fallen leaves softened the ground. Ferns arched across natural paths. The dim spaces between the trees offered refuge. Sky sat with her arms around her knees, head down, breathing in sharp gasps, willing the shaking to stop. She dripped with water and blood. Her head spun as she fought against the ravages of memory.

"Just breathe," she hissed. "Like in a competition...deep, even breaths...."

Far above the tossing branches, thunder cracked again like the sky had shattered open.

Again, horses screamed in fear. Sky forced herself to stand, steadied her spinning mind, and stumbled toward the horses; she would not leave them to the Nightmare...she would be safe with the horses...warm in a stable....

She staggered forward, shivering, shaking her head repeatedly, trying to make herself think despite the cold and pain. Abruptly, the woods ended at a white board fence. Past the fence lay a wide pasture with at least ten more horse fields and three barns beyond that.

Refuge. Warmth. Safety.

Above, the sky roiled grey with splinters of brilliant light flashing downwards. In the field before her, a stallion, gleaming unearthly white in the flashes of lightning, raced back and forth. His mane and tail billowed behind, flowing majestically as the animal reared and pawed the half-lit air.

Terror. Defiance.

Sky's head was thick with cold, but even half fainting, she was determined to save the creature. Save him from the Nightmare.

In the far field horses tossed their heads, racing wildly or crowding into three-sided sheds. In a corner connecting four fields, a huge tree lay across the grass, its trunk split wide, its wood black and smoking.

Lightning strike! So close...

Before her, the white horse pawed the grass and neighed defiance. Then the lightning zig-zagged down again, cracking open the air, sending every horse into panic again. The others had sheds. Shelter. Refuge. The white horse was alone in the field.

"It's okay...*I'm coming!*" Sky's voice was a thin whisper. She held her hands to her head, trying to stop the shivering, clamp down on the sensation that the ground wanted to spin away from her.

For a moment she thought she heard a voice calling out, but she couldn't distinguish any words. They didn't matter anyway.

The rain streamed the blood from her skin, leaving behind angry red welts. Her bones felt like rubber, but she didn't care. All that mattered now were the terrified horses – and above all, this perfect, white horse.

Somehow, she climbed the fence boards like a ladder and stood weaving slightly on the thick post as her endless hours of gymnastic training took over.

That voice again. *Who...?*

Sudden dizziness caused Sky to begin to fall, but with a surge of determination, she caught herself and turned the downward rush into a cartwheel along the thin boards. It was just like the balance beam, just like the times she was so hungry or sore she could hardly stand, but the Nightmare insisted she make a good showing – impress the people who watched her and would congratulate him.

There was that shouting voice. She would show what she could do...

The competition...yes...the competition... Sky finished the routine, only vaguely aware of the clicking cameras and flashing lights. This balance beam seemed too narrow, but she wouldn't fall. She never fell. Instinctively, Sky finished with an arms-wide dismount. There was no applause. Sky frowned and looked around. No...not a competition.... The white stallion. She had to protect the horse...

But she needed just a moment to catch her breath, to stop the shaking. In the far field she could see two men, fighting against the wind, pulling horses toward a barn. That was good, Sky thought blearily. The horses should be in the barn. They were all going into the barn. She should go too.

She would catch the white horse and bring him, too. She would ride him to safety.

Sky took a few uncertain steps and felt her trembling legs going out from under her. As she slid down into the thick mud, she heard that distant voice calling, screaming. *Must be one of the girls at the competition.* She should get up, but her legs just wouldn't do it. She could hear the Nightmare's footsteps. He was coming. He would be angry...she struggled to stand, but sank again, tears running down her face.

She pushed her hands into the mud, trying again to force herself to her feet. Hadn't she done her routine already? What did she have to do now?

Looking up she saw long, white legs in front of her...horse legs. The white horse. How could she have forgotten? Sky laughed and looked up at the rain-gleaming chest and long neck of the stallion.

"You came for me," she whispered and held up her hand. He dipped his nose, brilliant white that shaded to smoky black around his eyes, nostrils, and lips, and nuzzled her head.

"Yes, we have to go now," Sky said clearly. Above, thunder roared over them.

The horse snorted and his eyes rolled. His legs quivered and he stamped a fretful hoof.

"S'okay!" Sky mumbled. This time she forced herself to her feet. For a moment she leaned against the horse's chest, arms around his neck. She smelled his wet animal smell, felt his heart beating and the throbbing warmth of his life.

"I'll help," she said into his neck.

Her hands slid across his dripping coat, surprised that even so wet, it felt velvety to her. Grasping his mane, Sky pulled him around to face the barn. "You'll feel better inside," she croaked. "You'll be safe there. No nightmares..."

The horse jerked his head and his hooves danced dangerously close to her. Sky held on to his mane but looked down stupidly. In the distance, someone was screaming or shouting or something. That wasn't right.

"Come on," Sky said to the horse, and tugged his mane again. She felt his resistance, and laughed. "No, no, no," she said. "You have to listen to me. You need to get somewhere warm...so do I...."

The horse suddenly nuzzled her head and the flash of lightning seemed to highlight his white forelock and bounce in a long streak from his head. When it touched her, she felt a wave of strength and warmth.

"That's better," she whispered. "Good boy...."

Somehow, leaning heavily against the horse, Sky managed now to put one foot ahead of the other. Step by step, through the rain and sucking mud. She heard a man shout, and her stallion jerked back. But she held on, whispering hoarsely, that he must come with her.

The Nightmare and the Unicorn   53

She was distantly aware that a man came out of the rain and with a jumble of words she didn't understand, slipped a rope around the horse's neck. The white stallion didn't like it and reared.

"Be careful of him," Sky advised. "He's... he's..."

It was odd how sick she felt suddenly, how everything was dipping and swirling around her....

With a soft, "*Oh...*" Sky sank down into the mud between the horse's thrashing hooves. She saw him above her for an instant before her eyes fluttered shut and she sank into cold darkness.

Chapter 5

Horrified, Athena backed away from the fence. The horse...that poor girl had collapsed under the horse. Was she crazy? Why hadn't she listened when Athena screamed to be careful, to get out of the field? And now the girl looked like she might be dead...and the horse was rearing...

Frozen, Athena opened and closed her mouth, trying to scream. Like a nightmare, no sound came out.

Then Neil McClelland came...vaulting over the fence...throwing a rope around the thrashing horse, pulling it away.

With a sob of relief, Athena saw him scoop the unconscious girl into his arms and run toward the gate, and then head towards his home. Athena spun on her heels and stumbled down the path, through the pelting rain. The image of the girl sliding under the horse's hooves played over and over in her mind.

Almost whimpering, she slammed into her house.

Her mom was stretched out on the sofa, reading. She could hear the clatter of dishes from the kitchen.

"*Mom!*" Athena tore into the living room. "I just saw...*I saw*...!"

"You're getting the floor wet." Her mother put down her book and frowned suddenly at her daughter's expression. "What did you see?"

"This girl...she was nearly killed!" Athena tried to keep her voice from trembling.

"What? Who? Are you all right?" Her mom jumped to her feet and rushed over, eyes flashing over her daughter. "Daniel! *Daniel!* Where is a man when you need him?"

"Filling the dishwasher," Athena's dad said coming into the hallway. "What's the uproar?"

"Will you *listen!*" Athena carefully set her camera down on a side table. Her hands were shaking, but being home made things seem calmer, safer. "I saw a girl nearly killed just now."

"*What girl?*" her dad demanded.

"*Are you all right?*" her mother said at the same time.

"I'm fine," Athena pushed her mom's hand from her cheek and plunked herself onto the worn sofa. "I don't know who she is. I've never seen her before. Except for this morning." Athena paused, frowning, remembering the first glimpse she'd had of the girl. The kid had been on Stoltz's fence, leaning toward the horses. The girl was clearly crazed, whoever she was.

"What happened?" her dad asked again.

"I was taking photos out in the woods by McClelland's pastures," Athena explained. "Then I spent some time trying to get a good shot of the clouds and lightning. You know, for that Internet contest. Then this girl came crashing out of the woods, got up on the fence and started a really weird gymnastics routine – like she was in a gym instead of out in the middle of the country on top of the fence."

"Who is she?" her mother persisted. "There aren't any new families around, are there, Daniel?"

"Mom! There are no new families! Will you listen?"

"I am listening, Athena. So, don't scowl at me."

Her mom's face was turning pink, Athena saw. And her own was probably getting beet red. Just count to ten. Taking a calming breath to center herself, Athena continued. "I took a whole lot of pictures while she did this routine in the pouring rain. It was so beyond strange. Then she jumped off the fence…she didn't look very good," Athena frowned. "Kind of stumbled. But then one of McClelland's horses galloped over to her – just like a big dog – and started poking at her with his nose. I screamed and she didn't even notice. She just stood up and started pulling the horse toward the barn. Neil must've heard me because he ran over. And then the horse started rearing and the girl collapsed. I don't know if the horse killed her or what." Athena took a shuddering breath.

There was a moment of stunned silence.

"What did you do?" her mother asked.

"I came home," Athena said. She would *not* cry. "What was I supposed to do?"

"Help. You were supposed to help," her dad said. "Let's go."

"But, I..." Athena began and then snapped her mouth shut at the look in his eyes.

They threw on their coats and hurried out the door. Her dad led the way across the back yard to the gate between their property and McClelland's acres. Athena trailed behind, not sure if she was most angry or most embarrassed. It wasn't her fault the girl had collapsed, was it? Her parents were so typically not getting it.

Then she flushed with shame. She had gone home because of that huge, dangerous horse. Athena hurriedly blinked back some rebellious tears and kicked at the straggling weeds. Neil was there anyway – he didn't need her help. And now her dad was disappointed in her. The sick feeling in her stomach grew. Didn't he get it?

The rain was still sheeting down when her dad rapped hard on McClelland's door. It took only seconds for Neil to throw it open. His weather-beaten face showed surprise, and then he looked past their shoulders to the road.

"I thought you were the paramedics," he said.

"Athena saw the girl fall," her dad explained. "Can we help?"

"No, I..." Neil's eyes fixed on Athena's mom. "Come on in," he said. "It'd be good to have a woman here. The girl's unconscious, but if she wakes up..."

Athena noted the sparkle in her mother's eyes as she swept into Neil's enormous living room. The girl was lying on a sofa, eyes closed, face dead white, and her breathing hard and fast. She moaned and cried out, thrashing her arms as though she was falling.

"No! No...don't..."

Now Athena truly felt a rush of shame. She would have abandoned the poor kid. What kind of low-life human being did that make her? Determined to make up for her behavior, Athena first hovered over the girl as her mom tucked up the blankets more securely and made soothing sounds. The comforting murmurs didn't seem to make any difference to the girl's distress.

"Do you know who she is?" Neil was asking her dad.

"No idea," he replied. "Athena, do you know this girl?"

Athena shook her head. "I saw her for the first time this morning – over by the Stolz's pasture. Looking at the horses. But..." There was something. Athena frowned trying to remember. All she could recall was the sight of the girl leaning toward the horses with Judy Whitmore's awful dog beside her.

That was it!

"Judy Whitmore must know her," Athena said. "Her dog, Moose, was with the kid this morning."

"Does anyone have Judy's number?" Neil asked.

"No," Athena's mom said a bit sharply. "Judy keeps herself to herself."

It was then that the thin wail of a siren punctuated their anxious voices. Everyone froze and looked toward the wide picture window. To Athena, the moments became surreal as individual expression washed from everyone's faces. Neil pivoted on his heel and tore out of the door. Through the window, Athena saw him run down the long driveway to wave in the ambulance. It pulled up close to the house and two blue-shirted paramedics, a man and woman, swung out of the cab. Neil spoke to them quickly, gesturing toward the house.

The girl cried out again, "*No, don't! Don't...!*" Her voice subsided to a mumbling whisper.

"It's okay, sweetheart," Athena's mother crooned. "You're safe. There are no horses here."

"*Horses, the horses....*" The girl began to weep, dry keening sobs.

Involuntarily, Athena stepped back, terrified. Ready to sob, too.

The paramedics came in then, carrying a black bag full of medical equipment. Athena backed up against a bookcase gripping her own fingers really hard so she wouldn't cry out. Her mom and dad and Neil stood at the sides and back of the sofa, out of the way.

The woman took out a stethoscope, warmed it a moment in her hand, and then slid it under the neck of the girl's shirt.

"Hi honey," the medic said in a calm, friendly voice. "My name's Tania and I'm here to make you better. Heartbeat's regular," she said with no change of tone. Her partner tapped the information into some kind of tablet.

Tania took the girl's blood pressure while her partner called the hospital.

"Maybe if you gentlemen could step outside," Tania said. "There's blood on the girl's shirt and I need to check for wounds."

Neil and Athena's dad retreated to the kitchen. Athena's mom came over to the bookcase and stood beside her daughter, arm around her shoulder. Athena leaned her head against her mom, glad for once that she was there.

The paramedic undid the girl's shirt and paused a moment before her hands gently felt across the girl's prominent ribs.

"Evidence of past trauma," the woman said, her voice as dry as paper. "Possible malnourishment. No apparent new injuries other than scratches and superficial bruises." She felt down each of the girl's legs and then apparently satisfied, redid the buttons on the girl's shirt and pulled the blanket over her.

Her partner reported it all to the hospital staff. A buzzy voice that he seemed to understand responded. At that moment, the girl's eyelids fluttered open. Her eyes met

Athena's across the room and then darted around, taking in the room and the people. When the paramedic looked down at her, the girl's lids drifted closed. Athena was sure she was completely awake. Why was she just lying there? Why didn't she say something?

"Excuse me," the male paramedic called to Neil in the kitchen. "Are you the girl's guardian?"

"No," Neil said, coming back into the living room. "I don't know who she is, but I found her fainting in the field, hanging onto one of my horses. Did the horse injure her? Is she all right?"

"We didn't see any evidence that the horse stepped on her," the paramedic said.

"Thank goodness," Neil said. "We don't know who she is, but she might be staying with one of my neighbors."

"We need to contact the girl's guardian. She should go to the hospital and we need permission to treat her."

"I'll go get Judy," Athena said loudly. She couldn't stand this creepy room with the creepy girl who was pretending to be unconscious. And she couldn't stand the even worse feeling of knowing her dad was disappointed in her for abandoning the kid just because she was scared herself.

Before anyone could say anything, Athena went out the door. The rain had slowed to a soft drizzle, and the thunder and lightning moved into the far distance. The few horses left in the pastures were no longer dashing around madly. On the driveway outside the house, Athena stopped. The long way to Judy's farmhouse, by the road, was safer. The shorter, faster way led across the horse-inhabited fields. Time was probably important.

"Just whistle a happy tune, and no one ever knows you're afraid..." The whistle came out in a breathy hiss as Athena awkwardly climbed the fence into the pasture and only stumbling once, walk-ran across the muddy grass. On the far side, a chestnut mare cropped grass now that the storm had passed. Athena watched her from the corner of her eye, forcing the watery-weakness to stay in her arms and chest and not spread down to her legs. She could not collapse; she had to redeem herself.

Unattacked, Athena made it to the corner of the pasture. She had gone along the path on the far side of the fence a bunch of times and knew where to turn away to avoid the thicket of blackberries that made the woods so hard to get through. Finally, she was running across Judy's park-like lawn toward the yellow farmhouse. Hardly able to breathe, Athena tore up the back steps and hammered on the kitchen door.

"Ohhh" she moaned. She had forgotten about Moose. The monster dog leapt against the other side of the door, barking and charging.

Ready to eat her.

Ready to tear her to pieces.

She had to be having a heart attack because her heart was galloping against her ribs and she wasn't sure she could breathe.

"With her last gasp..." Athena declared, lifting her hand and pounding again on Judy Whitmore's door.

Chapter 6

Moose heaved up on his hind legs, leaned forward on the door, and barked ferociously through the glass. Cold terror squeezed the back of Athena's neck and sent icy lightning through her midriff.

"Just breathe," she told herself. "The dog can't get you." She refused to think about what would happen when the door opened. A second or two later, Moose was hauled down.

"No! Bad dog! What's gotten into you?" Judy Whitmore scolded. "Sit!"

The dog subsided to a reluctant sit, grumbling so loudly in his throat that Athena could still hear him outside. The door opened. Moose did not move.

Panting herself, Athena blurted out, "Please...that girl who was with Moose this morning...she's been hurt."

The woman stared at her uncomprehending for a moment. "Sky?" she asked finally.

Athena looked at her in confusion. "The skinny kid. Younger than me," she said tentatively. "Do you know her?"

"But she left! She and her mother left!"

Athena shook her head. "No! The girl I saw with Moose this morning was attacked just a few minutes ago by Neil McClelland's new horse. She's unconscious! The paramedics want to rush her to the hospital. You have to come!"

For a bare few seconds, Judy simply stared at Athena, and then abruptly went into action. With a quick order for Moose to *Stay!* she grabbed her keys from a hook rack behind the door and hurried out, pulling the door shut behind her. Moose howled a protest, but Judy ignored him.

"We'll drive over," she told Athena, leading the way to the garage.

Judy gunned the car. Athena gripped the armrest as Judy wheeled around the corners to where Neil McClelland's long driveway joined the road. Athena was bursting with questions, but after one glance at the woman's taut face, she didn't dare ask. Like everyone else in the neighborhood, Athena knew that Judy Whitmore and Neil McClelland had once been together, but they hadn't spoken in a dozen years. No one knew why.

Judy cranked the steering wheel to swerve past the ambulance, driving over a flowerbed and the smooth lawn before pulling back onto the gravel driveway as close to the front door as was possible. She yanked on the brake, jerked out the key, and slammed out of the car.

Athena took a steadying breath. "I've been on slower carnival rides," she muttered, and then ran to catch up – she did not want to miss a second of this soap opera.

Inside Neil McClelland's house, the scene was practically the same as when she'd left. The kid lay unmoving on the sofa with the paramedics leaning over her while the other adults hovered at a safe distance.

"Judy! Thank goodness you're here!" Athena's mom cried dramatically.

When Neil's eyes fastened on Judy Whitmore, his lean face took on a look of hard wood; he let his breath out slowly from between clenched teeth. Athena wished she could snap that picture.

Judy ignored him and everyone else, going straight to the girl on the sofa. Her eyes were still closed but Athena was sure that the kid was very conscious. Maybe the medics thought so too because the female paramedic had been kneeling beside the sofa, taking her pulse, and talking to her softly.

When she saw Judy, she stood up. "Are you this child's guardian?" she asked.

"I'm her great-aunt," Judy replied. "Her mother left her in my care."

Athena caught the slight flicker of the girl's eyes – she was definitely awake. No one else had noticed though. Would her next move be a slow flutter of the eyes and then an artistic moan? Athena was seriously curious about how the kid was going to fake this one. Crossing her arms and leaning against the bookcase once again, Athena was prepared to be entertained.

"We want to take her to Snohomish General Hospital," the medic continued.

"How badly is she injured?" Judy asked.

The medic hesitated. "There are no obvious injuries," she said. "But the child has multiple superficial abrasions, been chilled through, and attacked by a horse. She is probably dehydrated. We want to make sure she's completely okay."

At this point Athena suffered a shock. Without any warning, the girl's eyes came wide open and she sat up. "I'm fine," she said. "I don't need to go to the hospital. The horse didn't hurt me at all."

"Take it easy, honey," the medic put out a hand to support the girl, but she ignored it and stood up. Athena could see that the girl's legs were shaking and that her face was dead white – but she stood up anyway.

"I'm fine," she repeated. "Could we go home, Aunt Judy?"

Her great-aunt looked her over like she was buying a dubious horse, and then flipped her car keys in her hand.

"Yes, let's go, Sky," she said.

"Wait!" the medics said almost in unison. "We need some information."

"I can't give you any," Judy snapped. "My guardianship of Sky is extremely recent, and I know nothing of her medical history. If she's as shaken up as you say, she needs to be at home and in bed, not helping you fill out forms. Neil, seeing as her injuries took place on your property, at the hooves of your horse, and you called the medics, you can be responsible for their bill. Goodbye, everyone."

She put her hand on the girl's shoulder – Sky's shoulder – Athena corrected herself, and the two walked out together, both ramrod straight.

"Well, I don't know which one has the bigger poker up her backside," Athena's mom commented, aggrieved.

Beside her, Neil McClelland's wooden face twitched. To Athena's amazement, he began to laugh.

*   *   *

In the car, Judy's stiff face softened slightly. "Are you really okay?" she asked.

Sky nodded without meeting her eyes. "I'm cold and I got scratched up in the woods," she said, "but nothing else hurts particularly."

"I don't suppose your mom has health insurance?"

"No. Nothing." Sky closed her eyes and slumped back in the seat.

"Where is your mother?" Aunt Judy asked, her voice deceptively mild.

Sky kept her eyes shut, but her breathing speeded up. She felt so sick and shivery – where was her mom? Why did her mom's great ideas always go down the toilet?

"Sky," Aunt Judy's voice was sharper, "where is your mother?"

"She left," Sky said. "To look for work."

"Do you have her number? Can you call her?"

Sky shook her head. Her mom had thrown her phone out the car window the day they'd left. "She doesn't have a phone anymore."

Aunt Judy pulled into her driveway and stopped the car before turning to look at the girl. Over her simmering anger, she felt a slight jolt of pity. Sky's face was a sickly shade of white and she was shaking. It wasn't her fault that fourteen years later, Lindey was still pulling stupid stunts.

"Let's get you to bed," Aunt Judy said.

She walked behind the girl, ready to catch her if she fell, but Sky's back stayed painfully stiff and if her steps were slow, they didn't stop. Aunt Judy waited outside the room, while Sky stripped and climbed between the sheets. Moose jumped up on the bed beside her.

"*Down!* You stupid animal," Aunt Judy ground out.

"No," the girl whispered. Her voice was as close to tears as Judy had heard it.

"He's not allowed on the furniture and he knows it," Judy snapped. "*Down!*"

Head hanging, Moose crawled off the bed.

"Nursing isn't exactly my forte," Aunt Judy said. "I'll get you some hot soup and then you can sleep. I have a lot of work to do so I'll expect you to keep quiet unless you need something. Can you do that?"

"Yes," Sky said. She stared at the ceiling and didn't move.

With a stern look at Moose, Judy went downstairs and filled two bowls with canned soup. After a zap in the microwave she put the hot bowls on plates with spoons, and then as an afterthought, added a handful of saltine crackers and a cookie to each, and carried them both upstairs.

Sky's eyes were shut, but Judy was sure she was awake. She put a bowl of soup on the stand beside the bed and carried the second with her into her office – she could eat and read emails at the same time. And she was close enough to hear if the girl called out. It was not a surprise that a moment later she faintly heard the soft clink of the spoon on the bowl.

Later, after the girl had had a chance to sleep a bit, she would find out where her mother had disappeared to. Judy's fingers drummed lightly on the edge of the desk. Lindey's first disappearance had cost her unbearably. Family was family, but pay again for her niece's irresponsible behavior, she would not.

*   *   *

Sky slept for several hours, awakened finally by afternoon sunlight slanting through the window and falling over her face. This time, awareness of her surroundings came much more quickly. The brief warmth of knowing she was safe from the Nightmare was followed by a rush of terror. Aunt Judy now knew that her mom had abandoned her. Sky recognized the look that had hardened on her great-aunt's face. Anger. Accusation. Realization that she'd been tricked. Sky had seen the same ugly expression on some of the Nightmare's victims.

With her stomach turning to slow ice, Sky wondered what her great-aunt would do about it. Her fingers spasmed over the edge of the sheet, and she pushed one knuckle into her mouth, silencing any sounds of desperation. If Aunt Judy simply made a phone call and turned her over to the state, the Nightmare would find her. He was brilliant at hacking records and surfing through online information – all part of his schemes and swindles. Or maybe her great-aunt might let Sky stay but punish her for her mother's absence. What kinds of punishments would Aunt Judy decide were appropriate?

Before Sky could lose herself in worry, Moose pushed open the door and heaved his front paws onto the bed, nuzzling her neck and face, bathing her skin with his hot breath and slurpy love. Sky relaxed. Moose was a happy dog. Aunt Judy might be strict, but if she was given to harsh punishments, Moose would slink around with his head down and his tail would hardly ever wag. Reassured, Sky hugged Moose.

It would be okay. It had to be.

Chapter 7

"So, you don't know where your mom went?" Aunt Judy asked again. She passed Sky a bowl of salad that had come from a cellophane bag.

Sky shook her head and forked some onto her plate. "No. She said she was going to look for work and would come back for me as soon as she had some money." Sky put down the bowl and reached for a bottle of dressing. "I think she wants to find a job in a stable...She thinks maybe being around horses will bring back her...her..."

"Her magic." Aunt Judy's fingers drummed on the table. "She won't find it again with lies. Did she tell you the legend? That our family was gifted with horse magic when my grandmother risked everything to save a unicorn." Her eyes gleamed with amusement when Sky all but rolled her eyes. "And you don't believe a word of it. Well, it doesn't matter now. The magic's washing away. Every year...every lie that's been lived... Your mom's lost it. I barely feel it anymore. And I suppose you've never felt even a tingle."

Sky felt a tingle all right – but it was resentment. She didn't believe in that fairy story, even though the horses had come to her. Unbidden the thought rose...maybe...? Angrily, she banished the craziness. The Nightmare caught his victims by offering the hope of something too good to be true. She had watched and learned. Fantasy, no matter how she longed for it, would never trap her. She could learn about horses without the help of a unicorn.

During dinner, her great-aunt had been trying to make a stilted conversation with Sky about her friends and school. Sky answered carefully – if her great-aunt found out where she had come from, if Judy called the school or her mom's old job, someone might alert the Nightmare. He was so smooth and charming with his expensive suits, easy laugh, and cold, cold eyes...Sky shivered and in spite of herself, twisted her fingers.

"Does your mom have any friends around here that she keeps in touch with?" Aunt Judy persisted.

Sky shook her head. "She didn't tell me about any. May I be excused, please?"

Aunt Judy sat back and eyed her consideringly. "You seem to be a bright girl," she said at last. "I find it hard to believe that you have no idea where you used to live or where your mother is now."

"She promised to come back as soon as she could. She told me to help out in the house." Sky paused. Aunt Judy said nothing. "Should I clean up from dinner?"

"Yes, you might as well. You'll have to entertain yourself while you're here. I have a lot of deadlines to meet. And right now, I have a couple of errands." Aunt Judy stood up. "Lindey never did think through how her messes affected everyone else." At that, Aunt Judy walked briskly into the kitchen. Sky heard the clatter of her plate in the sink, then the back door opened and closed sharply.

Sky sat still for a moment, only the harsh, shallow breaths she took showing Moose her feelings. He pushed his nose into her lap and woofed gently.

"I know," she said. "Mom doesn't make great plans, but she does her best. She really does do her best, Moose."

The dog woofed softly again and looked at her worriedly.

"Forget it. I'm getting all wimpy," Sky said with a forced smile. "Let's you and me clean up."

Easy. Sky harvested a half a dozen left over French fries and a couple of chicken nuggets for her stash – she'd already eaten the saved

English muffin. While she hid the new plastic bags behind the books in her room, she left Moose to scour every morsel from the plates she put on the floor. After that, it took only a moment to put the bagged salad and dressings in the fridge, rinse the plates and cutlery and put them in the dishwasher. Sky debated whether to turn it on, but at only half-full that seemed wasteful.

"Tomorrow after breakfast," she told Moose.

Not knowing what else to do, and with the dog at her heels, Sky went outside. The car was still in the driveway, but there was no sign of Aunt Judy. Puzzled, Sky looked around the empty lawn and gardens. "Maybe she's visiting a neighbor," she told Moose, "but she doesn't seem like the visiting kind."

Without the exasperated eye of her aunt on her, Sky felt beautifully free. Even though it was past six o'clock, the sun had awhile to go before it would set. She breathed a big lungful of clean air – no city smog. From the pasture across the street, a horse neighed loudly, followed by another. She took a few steps in that direction – they seemed to call her. But another horse's call was stronger.

"*I'm coming!*"

Keeping an eye out for her aunt, Sky set off across the lawn. From long practice she stayed in the long shadows and moved as fluidly as she could without appearing to hide. It was better to look a little dumb instead of disobedient. Punishments for stupidity from the Nightmare had been harsh, but the punishments for defying him were...anguish. She had never given in to him, but just the same, Sky gritted her teeth at the memory of the times he had taken a belt to her or locked her in her room without food. But that was over. Instead of dwelling on those horrific times, she forced herself to concentrate on where she was going. The white stallion...she had to see him.

At a trot, she left the sweep of Aunt Judy's lawn and plunged into the coarse grass of the back pasture. The woods with their barrier of thorns lay before her – like Sleeping Beauty's castle, she thought grimly. But who was the wicked witch and who were the prince and the sleeping princess? Aunt Judy and Neil McClelland? Sky grinned at the picture of Aunt Judy in a princess dress and their angry neighbor in tights, tunic, and a feathered hat. And the wicked witch who caused it all? A picture of her mom suddenly leapt into her mind, so Sky shoved the whole pathetic idea out of her thoughts.

Picking her way between the spiked canes that spilled through the branches and spread into the grass, Sky approached the woods.

The trees towered before her, their branches rustling gracefully in the breeze – a pleasant conversation just beyond her hearing. A few early mosquitoes rose from the thicket and whined around her arms and head. She slapped at the insects and paced back and forth for a couple of minutes looking for a way in. Clearly, she could see the path where she had earlier crashed through the brambles, but even if some of the canes were bent, the net of thorns and spikes was still very much in place.

"So, Moose, do you think we'll have to go all the way around by the road?" Sky turned to talk to the dog, but he was no longer sitting behind her. A tiny, cold shock. Alone again. But why should she think Moose would just stay with her? Stupid. Incredibly stupid.

"Moose?" She hated how her voice wavered.

About fifty feet away, after a sudden crashing in the undergrowth, Moose's gigantic head thrust out between two bushes.

"*Woof!*" he announced, his tongue lolling in canine self-satisfaction.

Sky let out a long breath of relief and hurried toward him, but he didn't wait. With another "*Woof!*" he spun around and plunged back into the thick grass and shrubs.

"Moose!" In desperation, Sky ran after him. Twenty yards farther on, the undergrowth parted where a narrow path skirted a fence and led, thorn-free, into the woods. Moose sat waiting, tongue hanging out, panting gently with a smug grin on his face. Sky dropped her hand to his head and gently pulled his ears.

"Brilliant dog!" she whispered. He swished a soggy kiss across her hand, and then together, they trotted into the woods along the path that ended abruptly at the white board horse fence. The stallion stood in the center of the paddock, the setting sun gleaming across his white shoulders and proud head.

For a moment Sky simply stood at the fence, watching, marveling. She could see his protruding ribs, the hollows below his hips. Knowing to her core, the pain and neglect that had caused his bones to stick out like that, Sky felt a flash of rage. She gripped her hands into fists and felt the heat rising in her face. Beside her, Moose whined inquiringly.

"It's okay," she whispered. "We'll figure something out."

With a *huff* of agreement, Moose sank down onto the turf, clearly willing to wait while Sky looked after affairs here. During all this, the stallion's dark eyes never left her. Once or twice he snorted and pawed the ground, but he made no other moves. The sun shone across him giving the illusion of a filled-out form with a halo of light around his head. Drawn into his liquid black eyes, Sky slowly scaled the fence and dropped lightly to the other side. She stood motionless as the horse pawed the ground, danced back a couple of steps, and shook the long thick forelock from his eyes.

"Beauty," she whispered, extending her hand slowly. If only she had thought to bring some of the sugar lumps that overflowed Aunt Judy's sugar bowls. Instead she concentrated on sending the stallion waves of love, reassurance, and admiration. The horse whickered and again pawed the ground, head dropping as he took a few steps toward her.

Suddenly, a distant man's laugh rumbled through the air. The horse spun, neighed angrily and broke into a half gallop. Sky vaulted over the fence and crouched down in the trees' shadows. Staring through the gathering dark, she could dimly make out two figures, Neil McClelland...and her Aunt Judy. They were walking slowly toward the paddock, voices low as they talked.

The stallion neighed defiance and reared. Judy and Neil stopped by the fence and watched. Through the evening air, Sky clearly heard her great-aunt's voice. "So, this is your latest project. A little wild even for you, isn't he?"

Neil shrugged. "Maybe, but there's something about him I couldn't resist. Just look at those lines. Even half-starved he's more agile, stronger, and faster than any horse I've ever had in my stable. I heard he was culled from the Kiger herd in Oregon, but I've never seen any wild horse that looked like him. The fool who had him thought harsh treatment would break him."

Sky clenched her fists. The Nightmare had thought he could break her too. But he didn't. No one broke her – and no one would break this magnificent horse – no matter what she had to do to protect it!

Neil and Judy had been watching the stallion silently, but then Neil's voice cut through the air. "That horse cost me next to nothing at auction and I'll bet he'll make a really good profit."

"So, even with this glorious rescue, it's all about profit," Judy's voice mocked. "You may be getting older, Neil, but you aren't getting any smarter."

"You can't hold old mistakes against me!"

"Just watch me!" Judy retorted. "I shouldn't have wasted my time." With that, she lifted a hand and strode toward her own property, never once glancing back. Neil leaned against the fence and stared angrily at the stallion.

Moose whined softly in Sky's ear. In response she half-rose, faded backward into the shadows, and then ran lightly down the path toward the house. By the time Aunt Judy reached home by the laneway, Sky would be sitting on the sofa watching TV, the picture of the good little girl everyone wanted her to be.

Chapter 8

"I can't stand this," Sky muttered to Moose. "I want to check out the horses."

She had been hanging around the house all day, gnawingly apprehensive that any further trouble she caused her great-aunt that would spur the woman to "do something" about her – something that might alert the Nightmare to her whereabouts. And besides, she still felt worn out enough to sprawl on the sofa with a book lifted from Aunt Judy's overflowing shelves.

The lunch dishes had long-since been loaded into the dishwasher, and her great-aunt had stayed holed up in her office. Sky dropped the book carelessly on the cushions and quietly left the house. With Moose at her heels, she jogged down the driveway toward the field across the street.

As before, she stood up on the board fence, looking out toward the half-dozen horses. The teenage boy she had seen dancing with the mare the previous morning, was dropping forkfuls of hay into the pasture near the barn while the horses stood around the piles, contentedly nosing over the dried grass and crunching it between their big teeth.

If the boy saw Sky, he gave no sign of it. Methodically, with slow, strong grace he lifted the loose hay and forked it over the fence, moving a few feet each time so that no horse had to fight for its food. The black stallion leaned his head over the fence of his own pasture, clearly impatient for his share. When the hay was dropped in front of him, he huffed and bent his head gracefully to lip up his food.

Grudgingly Sky gave the teen kudos for his care that each horse was fed. And much as she wanted the feel of those bristly soft horse noses brushing her fingers, she would not stop them from eating. So, she simply watched and waited.

"Hi!" a nervous voice broke into her reverie.

Looking around, Sky spotted a girl with a camera slung around her neck, edging toward the fence. Even though she'd said *Hi* the girl's attention was wholly focused on Moose. To Sky's amazement, Moose stood stiff-legged, the fur along his spine lifting and his tail stretched out behind. Sky looked back at the girl – she radiated fear.

"Moose, sit!" Sky commanded. The dog hesitated until she pushed down on his bottom. Reluctantly, Moose sat. "If you're afraid," Sky told the girl sharply, "animals and bullies will always go after you – they'll try to hurt you."

"Which is why I am completely and utterly terrified," the girl said brightly. She climbed onto the top rail of the fence and sat there nervously. "Does he bite or eat people very frequently?"

Sky choked into laughter. "No, he's a big teddy bear."

"Possibly a teddy bear gone bad. I'm Athena Faviola," the girl said. "I was there when the horse attacked you. I went for your aunt."

Sky eyed her, reluctantly respecting that Athena forced a smile despite her obvious fear. "I'm Sky," she said finally, "and if you'll come down, I can introduce you to Moose."

"Oh, I'm not the formal type," Athena said. "Introductions, shaking paws...just doesn't do it for me."

Sky laughed. "So, are you going stay up there all day?"

"Pretty much. Until the dog leaves."

"How do you feel about horses?" Across the field, the horses were finishing their hay and the colt was trotting over toward them. A mare, the one that the boy had been riding, followed at a more leisurely pace.

Athena drew a long breath. "On the plus side, they aren't meat eaters. On the minus, they are too big and too stupid to know that I am too much of a coward to hurt them. There's that whole bully thing you mentioned." At that, Athena twisted to glance over her shoulder. "Oh, crap!"

"I'll move down the fence a bit and maybe they'll come to me." Holding her hand out over the fence, Sky walked down toward the corner of the pasture. After a moment's hesitation and a warning "woof" in Athena's direction, Moose stalked along behind her.

Leaning against the corner post, Sky held out both hands, longing for and mentally urging the horses to approach her. She closed her eyes and inhaled the green smell of spring, heard the soft flicks of tails and slow thud of hooves, and finally felt their soft noses brush her hands and arms. Her nostrils filled with their sweet, sweaty, horsey smell as she opened her eyes and ran her hands down the velvet of their necks, patted the strong muscles in their shoulders, and combed her fingers through the coarse hair of their manes. They glowed with health and confidence. These horses were loved and cared for. So filled with joy at their companionship, Sky did not hear the soft clicks of the girl's camera, or have any awareness of the heavy-footed boy striding across the field toward her. Moose's low bark alerted her. When she looked up at his flushed, angry face, the spell abruptly broke, and the horses drifted away.

"What are you doing to my horses," he demanded. "Get off my fence and stay away from them."

Sky stepped back, face burning in sudden rage.

"She wasn't doing anything to your precious horses," Athena called sharply, "unless rubbing their noses and talking sweet to them is going to ruin their tender psyches. Don't be such a jerk, Jeremy."

He turned his angry gaze toward Athena. "This is none of your business."

Athena hopped down from the fence, keeping a leery eye on Moose. "You sound like an adult," she said sweetly. "One of those really obnoxious adults who think they know everything and are much, much more important than stupid teens."

Jeremy's face turned even redder. "Athena," he growled, "you are the world's biggest pain."

Athena laughed. "Sky, this is Jeremy. Jeremy, this is Sky. Yesterday, Sky was attacked by Neil McClelland's big white horse, but that doesn't seem to have affected her crazy horse-lover thing."

Jeremy's eyes narrowed with interest. "That stallion attacked you? What were you doing?"

Sky glared at Athena. "He didn't attack me. I was trying to get him to the barn during the thunderstorm."

"I saw that horse when Neil unloaded him," Jeremy muttered. "Even half-starved he kicked apart the door of the trailer and broke the arm of one of the stable hands. Neil's the best horseman I know, even better than my dad, and he's not sure whether that stallion is too wild to train. You didn't go past the fence, did you?"

Sky nodded, chin up. "He was frightened," she said. "He knew I wouldn't hurt him, but Neil threw a rope over his neck and he panicked. That horse would never hurt me."

"You're loony tunes," Jeremy said brusquely. "You were lucky you weren't killed. And you'd better not forget this is private property – so stay away from my horses." With that, he turned on his heel and strode away across the pasture.

Sky let out her breath in a long hiss of frustration.

"Just ignore Jeremy," Athena said airily. "He's obsessed with his dumb horses."

"I saw him going through a kind of dance routine with that brown mare," Sky said reluctantly. "It was incredible. Beautiful and complicated."

"Whatever," Athena said, perching again on the fence while keeping her eyes firmly on Moose. "Before his mom died, the two of them were in dressage competitions all over the country. I have photos that I was able to sell online." She looked over at Sky waiting for her to be impressed. Nothing. Instead, the girl was still staring at the horses. "Everybody around here has horses, but it's not that easy to make money selling photos," Athena prodded.

"Maybe he needs some help," Sky said.

Appalled, Athena watched as she trotted along the grass verge, turned onto the gravel lane that led to Jeremy's house and with Moose at her heels, headed toward the barn.

"She *is* loony tunes." Leaving the protection of the fence, Athena glumly plodded after Sky. An opportunity for fame and fortune should never be ignored, and a plan, brilliant in its conception and possibilities, urged her forward.

Yesterday, through one dazzling photograph, Sky had become the miracle to make Athena's ambitions possible. And she was not the genius to let another such chance slip away.

*   *   *

When Sky passed a clump of trees, the barn lay to her left with the house straight ahead. She hesitated, unsure where Jeremy had gone. A man with unkempt beard stubble sat on a stump by the pasture smoking a cigarette, his back slumped and elbows resting on his knees. When he glanced her way, his eyes had a blurry look that Sky recognized – too much alcohol. She'd watched the Nightmare get his victims into that state often enough.

"Can I help you?" the man mumbled.

"Is Jeremy here?" Sky asked. Cautiously she kept her distance.

With the hand holding the cigarette, the man pointed toward the barn. Ashes caught in the fitful breeze and drifted into the grass. "He's in there." His voice was dull, but not unfriendly. "Here, I'll help you find him."

He got to his feet slowly, as though his body ached. "Are you a friend of Jeremy's?" the man asked. "I'm his dad, Roger Stolz."

Sky shook her head. "I just met him. I'm into horses...and I thought maybe he'd show me how he trains yours. I can help with the work."

Jeremy's dad looked at her. "You aren't very big."

"I'm strong," Sky retorted, "and I don't quit, no matter what."

The man smiled, his face lightening. "My wife was a skinny thing like you," he said. "She didn't give up either. You stick with that."

Sky nodded. "I will. So is Jeremy around?"

He sighed, seeming to forget her. "Marie hated it when people gave up," he muttered. "Jeremy's just like her. Doesn't give up. Nope," his dad said a little muzzily, "he doesn't give up....*Jeremy!*" he shouted suddenly. "Friend's here to see you!" He walked unevenly into the barn, his cigarette dangling unheeded from his fingers. "Jeremy!"

Sky waited outside, nose wrinkling a little at the acrid odor of cigarettes and stale liquor that trailed behind Jeremy's dad. Moose flopped down onto the ground beside her. As she waited, wondering if she should follow the man into the barn, an old dog paced out from behind a shed and ambled over toward them. Moose thumped his tail a couple of times but didn't rise. The dog sniffed Moose in impolite places and then shoved his nose into Sky's hand. After she'd scratched his ears, he dropped stiffly onto the ground beside them. Sky huffed out her breath impatiently.

Athena hovered well in the background, camera at the ready. From a cautious distance, she shot a few images of the two dogs, and then glanced around. Once she was as famous as her mother, people would be begging her to take their pictures and she wouldn't have to spend so much time trying to get a decent shot with idiots who didn't care whether they were immortalized in photos or not.

"*Jeremy!*" Mr. Stolz's voice echoed back from the barn's shadowy interior. Sky could see no light within except the pinpoint of his cigarette. She could hear the rumble of the father and son talking, and then finally Jeremy came out into the sunlight. His dad headed into the house and the teenager scowled after him, and then strode over to Sky.

"Why are you hanging around here?" Jeremy demanded. "What do you want?"

"Jeremy," Athena interrupted with fake enthusiasm, "you used to be a nice guy. Why are you snarling when Sky just wants to get to know your stupid horses?"

"I'm not snarling," Jeremy protested, his face flushing again.

Athena raised her eyebrows, and Sky fought off the sudden desire to laugh at the boy's bewildered expression.

"I want to learn to train horses," Sky said before Athena could attack again. "And I saw you riding. I could help clean stables or groom horses, or whatever, if you'd teach me."

"I don't need help," Jeremy said shortly, "and I don't give lessons." He walked away and disappeared into the house.

Sky glared after him, bitterly swallowing her disappointment. "What did I expect," she muttered to Moose. "All pixie dust and rainbows?"

As she turned to head home, the dog suddenly bounded to his feet and barked. Athena whimpered in terror and back-climbed up the fence. The old dog raised his head and sprang clumsily to his feet too, barking sharply.

"What is it?" Sky demanded as Moose whined and woofed at her. The old dog erupted into a rising crescendo of barks and Moose added to the din, running a few feet toward the barn and then backing up again. The door to the house swung open and Jeremy glared at them.

"What are you doing?" he yelled.

"*Ohmygosh!*" Athena screeched and pointed toward the barn. A thin wisp of smoke trailed from the top of the open doors. In the shadows beyond that, Sky saw a flicker of flame.

"Your barn's on fire!" she yelled at Jeremy. Without thinking she ran toward the blaze. *Were there any animals in there?*

"Dad!" Jeremy bellowed. "Fire!"

He tore after Sky, moving incredibly quickly for someone who looked so big and clumsy. Just inside the door, flames licked through a pile of hay on the cement floor. Smoke rose to cloud the ceiling as threads of glowing red floated in the breeze. Flames spat and crackled, dancing faster and higher through the hay. Jeremy yanked a fire extinguisher from the wall and aimed it at the smoldering hay. Sky grabbed a horse blanket from a stall and started beating and smothering the floating wisps of burning straw. A moment later, Jeremy's dad ran in, a hose spraying from his hands.

Behind them, Athena snapped pictures and the dogs barked and howled.

The water skittered hay and grass across the cement floor. Some pasty black ash. Some still glowing red. The smell seared Sky's lungs and she coughed, hacking through the smoke. Arms aching, she swung the blanket onto the red hay until all the strands were muddy black and the floor streamed gray-brown water. Beside her Jeremy paused and wiped his arm wearily over his face. Legs trembling, Sky folded her scorched blanket and laid it over a stall door, then wiped her mucky, wet hands on her jeans.

"That was close," Mr. Stolz said. He twisted the water nozzle to "off" and awkwardly began looping the hose around his arm.

"Yeah, Dad," Jeremy shouted. "And it was your cigarette that set the fire! What if the horses were in here? What if...." He broke off with a sob and turned away.

"Now, wait a minute!" Mr. Stolz dropped the hose and tried to catch Jeremy's arm.

But Jeremy shook him off and flung himself out of the barn. His dad swallowed and rubbed his hands over his face, barely aware of the two girls staring at him.

A long, heavy sigh escaped from him. "What is wrong with me?" he muttered.

"There's no real damage. Nothing was hurt," Athena offered timidly.

Mr. Stolz looked at the girls, as if suddenly remembering they were there. "Not this time," he said and followed Jeremy into the house. The door slammed behind him.

Chapter 9

With the door slammed so hard, the house looked like Sky felt – closed up and silently terrified. She rubbed her fingers into her hair to clear those thoughts and returned her gaze to the shambles in the barn.

"Well, that was exciting," Athena said. "But not such a good time that I can't leave it behind. I'm going home. Are you coming?"

Sky shook her head. "I'm going to clean this up first."

Athena sniffed. "Not me. I don't do hard labor. Besides, I've got some things to do. Maybe I'll see you tomorrow?"

Sky nodded. "Whatever."

"*À demain.*" Athena waved and giving Moose a wide berth, headed down the lane toward the main road.

By the half-light from the wide doors, Sky moved slowly through the barn, gazing longingly at the clean stalls and the horse tack neatly hanging on pegs. A broom was propped against a wall, so she carried it back to the site of the fire and swept the mess of charred straw into a soggy pile. Not knowing where to dispose of the debris, she reluctantly returned the broom to its place and left the blackened mound.

"Come on, Moose," Sky said and walked slowly along the grass by the horse fence. Feeling like she was being watched, Sky looked back quickly. Jeremy stood in the door of his house, staring at her. She raised her hand in a small wave and was glad to see him nod in her direction. Then he drew back, and the door closed again.

The late afternoon sun slanted across the landscape as Sky climbed the porch steps. She hesitated, hotly anxious whether she should knock or just walk in. The question was solved when Aunt Judy opened the door.

"I was beginning to worry where you'd gone," she said mildly. Her forehead crinkled and she sniffed distastefully. "What's that smell?"

Sky forced a bright smile. "I went across the road to look at the horses. They had a small barn fire."

Aunt Judy looked sharply across the road. "Any horses hurt?" she demanded.

Sky shook her head. "No. Or I wouldn't just be standing here, would I?"

Her great-aunt's eyebrows rose. "You ought to be standing in a shower." She stepped to one side and gestured toward the hallway. "Once you've cleaned up, you can tell me about it. Seems you've inherited your parents' love of all things equine."

"My parents?" Sky froze. "Did you know my father? Before he died?"

Aunt Judy nodded. "All his life. That motorcycle accident was a real tragedy and it left your mother stranded with six kinds of trouble and you on the way." She looked Sky over as if still perplexed about what to do with her.

"Can you tell me about my father?"

Aunt Judy frowned. "Don't tell me he was another of your mother's misguided secrets?"

Heat rose in Sky's face. Tamped down anger. Old hurts.

"I'd like to hear what you remember about him," Sky managed. She wanted to scream at her aunt, but she wouldn't give herself away. To carry the look of indifference, she moved slowly across the large kitchen, toward the hallway.

"During dinner, I guess." Judy picked up waiting pieces of chicken and a can of cream soup and dumped them in a frying pan. As it heated, she began stirring impatiently. "Two weeks," she muttered. "I have two weeks to finish my manuscript, but I need four."

Sky's anger flared again. She didn't give a rip about Judy's manuscript, but she'd had a lot of practice at gaining her own ends, so she left quickly and quietly. A few minutes later, clean and wet-haired, she returned to the kitchen and mutely took out vegetables for salad. She moved carefully – nothing banged as she laid the ingredients on the counter. Taking a paring knife from a drawer, she silently peeled and chopped.

It was almost pleasant. Before the Nightmare, a thousand years ago, she and her mom had made dinner together every night in their tiny, worn-down apartment. They'd been broke but a lot better off. The Nightmare's money and fancy house had not made them as happy as those scraped-together meals.

Aunt Judy took a bag of frozen vegetables from the freezer and dumped the contents into the skillet as well.

"Your father was basically a nice boy," she began without preamble, "but his mother was the silliest human being I ever had the misfortune to meet. When your grandfather died, she fell apart. And she kept telling Jimmy, your dad, that everybody else had life easy. That was how the trouble started."

Sky's hand stilled from chopping carrots. "What trouble?"

Aunt Judy tasted the stew and then made a face. Reaching for the salt, she dashed it in liberally before speaking again. "He and your mom wanted to get engaged, but he thought he needed to give her a big expensive ring, like he'd seen on...on someone else's finger." Judy's face hardened. "As though a ring matters. Money doesn't matter, Sky. Remember that. Money never matters without trust and compassion."

Sky gazed under her lashes at her great-aunt, her own chin stiff with agreement. The Nightmare's money hadn't mattered at all, even though her mom had thought it would make their lives better.

"So, when your mom became pregnant with you and wanted Jimmy to marry her right away, he stole money from Neil McClelland to buy her a ring. Your dad trained and rode sometimes for Neil – that's how he met your mom," Judy said. "Jimmy was a horseman through and through. Just not patient enough to build his own stable slowly the way Neil had."

"I...I didn't know that," Sky said. She hadn't known her dad was a horseman because her mom had refused to talk about him, except to say that he had loved them, and he had died. Sky hadn't known that he had stolen money either.

Both things made her throat tighten, but she never cried in front of people, so she whacked some zucchini instead.

"Then it got ugly," Judy went on. "Your mom told Neil and me that *she* had stolen the money – it was a very stupid attempt to protect Jimmy. She thought that because I was...I was close to Neil back then, that he would hold off prosecuting. She didn't know Neil," Sky's great-aunt said bitterly. "Nothing came between him and his bank account. He and Jimmy were a bit alike that way, although Jimmy was always generous with any money he did have."

"Then what happened?" Sky asked. She despised the quiver that rose in her voice, but Aunt Judy was stirring their dinner slowly, staring into the distance, and didn't seem to hear it.

"Within a week, Jimmy was killed in a motorcycle accident. Neil remained unmoved by your mother's situation. I thought she had stolen the money too – she said she did, after all. But I would have helped her sort it out," Judy said fiercely. "She never thought things through. Never! She ran away and I didn't hear a word from her until after you were born."

Aunt Judy's eyes swept over Sky. "I wrote her to come home, that Jimmy had left the money with your mom's brother-in-law, Roger. But she wouldn't come back," Judy said. "She said she didn't want to raise her daughter where there was no trust. Stubbornness, hurt pride, and no sense at all."

Sky stood statue-still, waiting for her thunderstorm of emotions to settle somewhere, anywhere.

"And I haven't seen her since then," Judy said. "I didn't even know where she was exactly – not until she dropped you into my lap." She gave the stew a vicious stir. "Sky, what kind of trouble is your mother in? I looked after her and her older sister, Marie, when their parents died. I'm half a mother to her." Aunt Judy turned toward her, her stern face suddenly anxious. "You have to tell me. What is going on, Sky?"

Sky breathed slowly and deeply, ripping a head of lettuce into shreds. It was like a gymnastics competition where she had to quiet her frantically beating heart and channel all her strength into the perfect performance. She raised her eyes to her great-aunt's steely grey gaze.

"I don't know," she said. "Mom said she was tired of California and decided to come up here to look for a job. Maybe..." Despite herself, a sob gripped her throat, but she wouldn't let it escape. Not now. Sky steadied her voice. "Maybe she just wanted to come home. I don't know anything else."

Sky lowered her eyes to the bowl in front of her. "The salad's done," she said. "Should I set the table?"

Later, when dinner was eaten, cleared away, and a mindless comedy was watched on TV, Sky escaped to her room. As she lay in bed, Moose yawned beside her and affectionately buried his nose in her hair. Her mind endlessly turned and rolled, thinking about what her great-aunt had told her. Her father had stolen, but he was generous. Her mom had lied to protect him, and then run away to save herself.

Sky stared at the ceiling, watching a spider spin a web. So, no real change. When life with the Nightmare had gotten too ugly even for her mom, they had run away and then lied to save themselves. A stab of fear made her breath ragged. Her mom's lies and running away had been disastrous before – why would this time be any different?

Moose heaved a contented sigh, stiffened his legs, and pushed his big paws against Sky's back. She rolled over to lay her cheek beside the big dog's forehead and with his foreleg draped over her shoulder, slipped into a dream.

The white stallion whinnied and reared against the fence that held him captive. Thunder and lightning split the night as Sky balanced precariously on the fence. Somewhere, the Nightmare laughed, and lightning forked through the night again, striking trees and knocking them down helter-skelter.

"Get back here!" the Nightmare called. "You'll be sorry if you don't!"

Thunder rolled. Lightning struck. The horse reared and tried to escape the death hurled at him.

Sky wanted to vomit. Her legs and arms hung heavy as lead, sodden with fear. She would run. She would tell a lie and she would escape.

The Nightmare held a rope and swung it around the stallion's neck. Too tight. Choking. The horse cried in terror...pleading. How could she leave the horse to the Nightmare's cruelty?

Sky allowed herself to fall from the fence into the field. Lightning struck around her. The air singed with fire. Flames licked up from the grass. Weeping, sobbing, she staggered toward the horse.

Watching lazily from a perch on a fencepost, the Nightmare chewed a straw like an old-time farmer and laughed uproariously as she struggled through burning grass and mud.

And then miraculously, as Sky began to fall, the horse dipped his head. A silver horn shone from his forehead. Gently, he touched her face.

"You are safe, Dear Heart," the horse whispered to her. "You are safe."

The stallion stepped back and reared. Lightning shot from his horn and struck the Nightmare full in the chest. The monster yelled his rage, fell backward, and shriveled into ash.

But his voice still whipped across the wind. "I'll be back!" he screamed. "You can't get away from me, Sky. I'll be back for you!"

Sky woke up abruptly, panting, shaking. She burrowed her fingers reflexively into Moose's fur and tried to quiet her breathing.

It was a long, long time before she slept again.

*   *   *

One of the things Jeremy had always loved about his attic bedroom was the view it gave him of the land around his home. Tonight, he pushed up the wood-framed window as high as it would go and leaned out – like a lord looking out over his domain.

The horses in the pastures below were settling in for the night, Molly lying in the grass with Rook still restless, and Prince Caspian standing guard on his side of the fence a few feet away. Firefly cropped up a last few mouthfuls of grass, but Lady and Fledge were in their sheds, heads hanging and one foot cocked up in sleep. He heard the soft *whooo* of an owl winging through the night and saw the silver ghost of a hunting coyote slip past the barn. The coyotes never bothered the horses, but they were a menace to any cats and chickens in the neighborhood. His own cat was safe in the kitchen.

Jeremy breathed in deeply, relishing the cool green smell of the air, but his lips thinned as he caught a wisp of stale ash from the barn fire. His big hands curled into fists and he thumped them briefly on the sill to beat out some of his frustration. If those girls hadn't seen the flames, the wooden barn could have burned to the ground. What was wrong with his dad? How could he have become so stupidly careless? This time they'd been lucky.

Looking out past his own fields, Jeremy could see the lit-up windows at the Faviola house. The TV was going in the living room and he could just make out Athena's form leaning into a computer screen in her upstairs bedroom. Her workstation was against the window so he saw her there a lot of nights as she did whatever with the million or so photos she took every day. He switched his gaze over to Judy Whitmore's as he saw an upstairs bedroom light blink out. That must be where that kid, Sky, was staying. Weird girl, definitely weird, but with a rush of gratitude Jeremy decided he owed her.

He was just turning back into his darkened room when there was a knock on his door.

"I'm going to bed," he called gruffly.

There was a moment's hesitation, then his dad said, "Maybe we could talk for a minute?"

In exasperation, Jeremy yanked open the door. "I don't know what we have to talk about. Even though it's spring vacation, my homework's all done. In case you're suddenly worrying about it."

Even in the half-light of the stairway's bulb, Jeremy saw the flush that darkened his dad's cheeks. "Jeremy...son...I just wanted to tell you, I've been thinking about what you said."

Jeremy stayed angrily silent. His father slid his hand up the door jamb, as if he was going to lean on it, and then shifted his feet and dropped his arm uncomfortably. His eyes met his son's. "You were right, Jeremy. It didn't just happen to me. I'm sorry I haven't been much help to you...and I'll try to do a little better." He took a deep breath. "Okay."

Jeremy watched as his dad turned and went back down the stairs. He wanted to call out, but the words wouldn't escape his throat. Finally, he returned to the window and stared up at the sky, remembering how his mom and dad had taken him out into the fields a thousand years ago and shown him how to find the Big Dipper shining above them.

"Star light, star bright," he whispered, then with a sigh of irritation, closed the window and went to bed.

114   Susan Brown

Chapter 10

The next morning was a repeat of the previous day. Sky woke up to the faint *tap, tap* of her great-aunt's computer keys in the next room. Moose had left the bed but was now staring at her with a dog's patient insistence, his snout about five inches from her face, and small, quivering whines rising from his throat.

Sky startled into alertness and then within a minute rolled out of bed. She dressed quickly, choosing her least dirty clothes. Later, when Aunt Judy emerged from her office, she would find out where she could launder her things. Later.

Following Moose downstairs, she saw that once again, her great-aunt had laid out a selection of breakfast foods on the counter. Sky shared her English muffin with Moose, gave him her nearly empty cereal bowl to lick out, and then again, made a muffin to put in her stash. She wondered briefly if she should conceal food outside, but decided that in the country there might be too many animals that would sniff it out no matter how careful she hid the cache. Besides, it seemed unlikely that Aunt Judy would knowingly lock her out the way the Nightmare had.

With soft footsteps, Sky went upstairs and slid the wrapped muffin behind a fat book on the shelf in her room, and then without her aunt ever hearing her, crept downstairs again. Whatever book her aunt worked on kept her safely focused – just like the Nightmare's schemes had completely absorbed him. Her only times of safety.

When the Nightmare was in the house but not working in his office, Sky stayed in her room. While he developed some new scam, she warily pursued her own plans. She liberated unnoticeable amounts of food for the bad times, tried to scrounge some cash for a getaway. She even sneaked into the Nightmare's lair and read file after file. He never caught her because she had perfected her façade – a submissive, blank-faced girl – but her hidden heart throbbed with rage. Steeled into determination, Sky never stopped looking for ways to destroy his schemes.

She'd deleted one or two contacts from his cell phone, dropped letters here and there into his shredder, and kept food secreted everywhere she could, so that when he decided to starve her, she stayed strong. When he ranted about the gremlins in his life, Sky kept her head down and smiled. She never stopped her whispering campaign to get her mother to walk away from the fancy house, the credit cards, and the terrifyingly cruel man.

So pathetic...so many tiny, useless ploys... but eventually Sky had won. Sort of.

Her own nightmares woke her nightly, often dripping with cold sweat. Her mother had bolted – gone AWOL. And Sky's endurance had been strained to the point she'd collapsed in the field. Not okay. So not okay. She had to get stronger and tougher. In case. Just in case.

With a bitter grimace, Sky wondered when the Whitmore women's famous unicorn would gallop to the rescue.

Methodically, she put away the breakfast foods, wiped the counter and added the dishes to the dishwasher, all the while thinking about what she should do next – thinking about what her great-aunt had told her about her father. He had grown up near here and he had been a horseman. That part was great, but Sky resolutely faced the fact that her father's theft, even if it had been for her mother, had been the first step that brought them into the Nightmare's world.

And where was her mom now? How long would it be before she thought they were safe and came back for her daughter? What if she didn't come back? What if she caved and called the Nightmare instead? Insane as it seemed to Sky, she knew her mother had never stopped hoping he would love them, would "wake up" and shower them with a good life.

Her mom hadn't figured it out – monsters of cruelty don't become Prince Charmings, Sky thought bitterly. And the only weapon she had was a single thumb drive with copies of the Nightmare's files. In the seconds before their flight, she had gone into his office and yanked it from his computer. She didn't even know if the copied files could harm him, but it was the best she had been able to do. If she had been sure, she could have gone to the police. But the Nightmare had so many "friends" and was so smooth and convincing, she feared that even the files would not be enough.

But it was all she had. Except for the famous Whitmore unicorn magic, she thought bitterly.

Sky pushed the dishwasher door shut with a snap and took a deep breath. It had only been four days. Her mom made mistakes, lots of mistakes, but regardless of what else she had left behind, she had never abandoned her daughter. Her mom would come back. For sure. Absolutely for sure. There was no point worrying about it.

With Moose at her heels, Sky strode out the kitchen door and jogged toward the narrow path to Neil McClelland's fields. She wasn't the only one who had been hurt, hungry, and frightened. The white horse drew her like the magic her mom had rattled on about. At the woods, she slowed to a walk, not wanting any crashing noise to startle the horse. *Her horse.* Stupid as it seemed, in her bones, Sky knew the white stallion was destined to be her horse.

At the edge of the pasture, Sky came forward slowly, climbing onto the first fence board. The horse watched, ears laid back and then flicking forward, muscles quivering across his chest and beautiful shoulders. She met his eyes, slowly held out her hands, and then looked to the side, not dominating – but offering her friendship. She filled her mind with images of her loving fingers stroking his arched neck and her warm breath floating over his nostrils.

The horse snorted and shook his head, lifting the long strands of his mane in the breeze. Sky waited, longing for that moment of magical connection. Moose lazily stretched and then heaved up so that his front paws and head also rested on the top board of the fence. The stallion snorted again, backed up a few steps, tossed his head and stared at them. The sun haloed across his head and mane. He was so beautiful and determined that, despite his too-thin body, she had to love him for the unbroken pride in his eyes.

The horse whinnied, a sound almost like a laugh, and slowly, step by step, moved toward Sky. His head bobbed with each footfall as he eyed her from every possible angle. A jay squawked from a branch. The stallion jerked, paused, huffed, and then slowly stepped toward her again. He stopped ten feet from the fence and pawed the ground.

"Hi," Sky breathed, turning up her palm. His neck stretched slowly toward her...and then...

"Hey boss, you want to move that new stallion?" A harsh voice thrust through the air. *"I ain't going near him by myself."*

Sky started, gave a soft cry, and stepped off the fence, back into the shadow of the trees. The horse whinnied angrily and spun, leaping forward into a gallop that took him around the perimeter of the field.

On the far side of the pasture, slouching glumly, stood one of the men Sky had seen struggling with the horses during the storm. Just now he was turned toward the barn, waiting instructions from a shadowed figure in the wide doorway.

"No, let's give him a few more days to settle down," Neil McClelland called. *"Check his*

water and make sure he gets some extra food. I'll try to get a halter on him."

As Sky watched, the hired man left with a shake of his head. Neil emerged from the shadow of the barn and strode purposefully toward the paddock, a worn halter dangling from his hand. He stood a moment, eyes narrowed against the sun, watching the stallion gallop and swerve. When the horse slowed, he climbed agilely over the fence and stood motionless, the halter held loosely in his two hands. Once again, the stallion erupted into motion. Eyes never leaving the gleaming horse, Neil waited for long minutes until the animal slowed and stood blowing and pawing at the far end of the field.

Breathless, Sky watched as Neil moved cautiously toward the horse, speaking softly, reassuringly. The horse shook his head and backed up, whinnying angrily, but Neil kept moving toward it. Finally, the stallion stood motionless, with only a quivering shoulder showing his agitation. Sky held her breath, waiting for Neil to hold out his hand to the magnificent animal.

But he didn't. At the last moment Neil shifted the bridle and tried to grab the stallion's mane while pushing the halter toward its head.

"No!" Sky cried and clapped her hands over her mouth. Moose whined.

The stallion reared, pulling himself from the man's grasp. His hooves slashed the air. Neil ducked and ran for the fence, vaulting over just as the horse charged him.

Enraged, the stallion whinnied his defiance and began circling the paddock again, stopping only to trample the halter into the churned-up earth. Neil stood by the fence staring at the horse, a frown puckering his forehead. Sky faded farther back into the woods, certain that no matter what she did, the horse would never come to her again today.

*   *   *

Once more, lunch consisted of canned chicken noodle soup with crackers, served today at the dining room table. Sky spooned up every drop and ate one third of the crackers on the plate. Half would have been fair, but the Nightmare had once knocked her clear across the room for being greedy when she had taken what she had thought was her share of the brownies her mom had made.

Her great-aunt frowned at her. "You're awfully thin for a girl your age. You don't do any stupid dieting nonsense, do you?"

Sky shook her head. *Not by choice.*

"Good. There's lots of bread and butter, or cereal if you want a snack anytime, and there are more English muffins in the freezer." Aunt Judy gestured vaguely toward the kitchen. "You need some meat on those bones, so help yourself to anything you fancy. I'll get some cookies and such next time I'm at the grocery store."

"Thank you." Sky smiled politely. "Sounds great."

Whatever else they might have said, was drowned by Moose's leaping to his feet and barking ferociously at the kitchen door. A firm knock echoed between *woofs*.

"Now what?" Judy tossed down her napkin, limped over to the door and then stopped, staring through the window. Carrying the dishes to the sink, Sky saw her aunt's lips thin.

"Moose, *sit!*" Judy commanded. Moose dropped to his haunches, sinking his head at the harshness of her voice. Sky felt her own stomach quiver in reflected anxiety, as with deliberate movements, her great-aunt opened the door halfway.

"Neil," she said, "this is an unexpected honor."

"Hello, Judy. I came to see how the girl is." Neil McClelland's voice sounded awkward, even to Sky's ears.

"She's fine," Judy said, opening the door wider. "No thanks to your horse. Come and see for yourself if you want."

"Thanks, I will," Neil said, stepping into the kitchen. He glanced over at Sky standing frozen by the sink, and smiled. "Good to see you up and around. Are you feeling all right now?"

Sky nodded. Suspicion, panic, gripped her.

"Good. Glad to hear it." Neil paused and cleared his throat. "So, what were you doing in that field anyway?"

Sky's heart hammered her chest. Had he seen her again this morning? *No...the storm... the screaming horses...mud...hanging onto the white stallion as though her life depended on it.*

She needed an explanation. Needed to deflect his anger. She smiled and smiled...

"I got lost in the storm," she tried. "I thought I was going toward Aunt Judy's house, but I ended up by your pasture." She raised her eyes to his and from long practice, let no negative expressions creep onto her face.

"And you couldn't tell the difference between a house and a pasture?" Neil's voice was faintly mocking. "You don't look that stupid."

"It was pouring rain, Neil," Aunt Judy interjected sharply, "and Sky's never been in the country before. Or are you setting up a defense for a lawsuit because your horse attacked her?"

"You know me better than that, Judy." Neil's brows drew together. Sky stepped back as Aunt Judy took a step forward. Her chin jutted and her eyes sparkled with anger.

"Do I, Neil? But you don't have to worry. Not everyone is as devoted to money as you are."

"That's not fair, Judy." His mouth pulled tight. "I just wanted to check on the girl, that's all." He looked back toward Sky and as he studied her, his eyes became intent. "Have I seen you before...? " he asked slowly. "Lindey!" he said abruptly and turned to Sky's great-aunt. "This is Lindey's daughter?"

Aunt Judy nodded confirmation; Sky didn't move a muscle.

"Okay...your mother worked for me once," Neil said awkwardly.

Sky eyed him, wondering if he would hate her because of her mother. Wondering if she would hate him because of how he handled the horse.

"Your horse is awfully thin," Sky said, anger at the stallion's mistreatment pushing all caution out of her mind. "If you feed him right, he won't try and attack you."

"Thanks for the advice." Neil retorted. "I didn't know you were an expert."

Sky met his eyes, her own now steely, ready for battle. "He's been hurt and starved. But you think you can just make him tame, make him do what you want because you're so smart and strong."

For a moment Neil looked furious, and then a slow smile slipped over his face. "You're a lot like your mother," he said. "She always said what she thought, too." The smile disappeared abruptly and he turned to Judy. "I can see that she is recovering just fine."

"Sky is all right," Judy said pointedly.

Their eyes met, locking in old anger. Silence stretched across the room, with neither looking away. Then Judy made a sound of irritation and pulled open the door, clearly signaling that she was done, and it was time for him to leave.

Neil took a folded paper from his pocket and held it out to her. "I've paid the paramedic charges. If Sky needs any follow-up, let me know and I'll look after the bills. At least I'm honest."

Judy shut her mouth into a thin line, glanced at the paper and nodded. Neil turned back to Sky. "I may drop by again...to see how you're doing. But stay out of my fields. You might not be so lucky next time."

He strode out. Judy shut the door with a snap, her face reddened as she turned on Sky. "What was that nonsense?" she demanded.

Sky lifted her chin. "That beautiful, beautiful stallion's ribs are sticking out – he's half-starved and he hates people. I don't blame him! Neil just tried to bridle him like it was nothing."

Judy shook her head in exasperation. "You also leap to conclusions like your mother. Neil's never mistreated a horse in his life – he saves his nastiness for people. Neil's taken dozens of horses from the horse rescue people – he looks after them, retrains them and gets them to people who'll treat them right."

"Oh," Sky said, her face flushing. "I didn't know...I mean...."

Aunt Judy smiled without much humor. "Don't worry about it. Neil McClelland brings out the worst in the Whitmore women." She turned toward the stairs. "Can you keep yourself busy for a couple of hours while I finish my weekly blog?"

"Sure." Sky stood waiting until Aunt Judy's slightly uneven footsteps signaled that she was in her office. Scooping the uneaten crackers into a plastic bag, Sky stole up the stairs and hid them behind the books, then with Moose at her heels slipped outside.

She considered returning to the white horse's pasture, but hesitated. Her run-in with Neil made her cautious. The man might be keeping an eye out for her.

Moose pushed against her, impatient for action. Sky looked down and with a small smile stroked his head.

"That horse needs someone to love him... and I can do that." She turned and stared in the direction of Neil's stables. "No way though that I'm adding to his problems. Moose, I have to learn more about horses – even though they all keep saying it's in my blood. And they think a unicorn will show up to make everything right." Sky paused. "I wish...but not holding my breath."

Sky walked slowly along the driveway, considering. Aunt Judy no longer had horses and her lame leg apparently made riding and training too hard for her. Except for Neil, Sky only knew one other person who could teach her. Asking for anything terrified her, but how else could she save the stallion? Stiff with determination, Sky headed across the road to Jeremy Stolz's stable.

She would learn everything – and save that perfect white horse by doing it.

Chapter 11

The colt was dashing madly about, kicking up his heels and half-rearing in the exuberance of being young. One of the other horses, a light brown mare galloped alongside him before stopping to grab mouthfuls of new grass.

Sky watched them, noticing that the mare, Molly, was absent. A couple of minutes later, she spotted Jeremy leading the horse from the barn and over to an empty training ring. He swung into the saddle and after allowing her to plunge and toss playfully, began the elegant, high-stepping dance of dressage. Sky held her breath. Horse and rider became a smoothly flowing team, their bodies in sync as Jeremy's light hands twitched and his body leaned into the complex ballet of Molly's patterned steps.

Sometimes they stopped and restarted a particularly complicated maneuver, apparently correcting flaws too minute for Sky to identify. Partway into the pattern, Jeremy's dad came out of the house and watched for a few minutes. Then he climbed over the fence into the ring and began talking with Jeremy, gesturing, and nodding. Sky saw that there was none of the teen's anger from the night before, just an intent expression in his eyes as he listened to his father's advice. Then he began the pattern again.

Unable to bear watching from a distance, Sky walked slowly along the fence to the training ring by the barn, longing to see more, apprehensive that they would order her away. Then what? She stayed motionless in the shadows of an overgrown bush, but Jeremy's dad noticed her. Instead of waving her away, he came over to the fence and smiled. Today he was shaved, and his eyes bore none of the muzzy, drinking look.

"I didn't get a chance to thank you for your help yesterday," he said. "If that fire had gotten out of control, it would have been a disaster for us."

"At least none of the horses got spooked," Sky said, carefully matching his smile. "It would have been awful if they'd been in their stalls."

"Yeah," Mr. Stolz said. "I saw that happen once, years ago. An electric wire sparked and set the hay on fire. It was daytime, so everyone was in there, trying to get out the horses. They were screaming and plunging but wouldn't leave their stalls unless they were blindfolded and trusted the person trying to lead them.

Terrible." He shook his head at the memory. "Hope I never see anything like that again."

Just then, Jeremy and Molly danced close to the fence. Mr. Stolz turned to watch, the grim look fading from his eyes as he smiled in pride. "Jeremy's won the west coast championships in both dressage and jumping for his age group," he said. "But since his mom became ill, he's not been competing. Now that he's working at it again, I hope he can win the national in a year or two. Maybe even make the Olympic team one day. He's got his mother's way with horses. She'd be real proud."

Sky's fingers curled tightly around the top of the fence boards. She controlled her breathing and forced out the words. Made them sound casual. "I want to be a horsewoman," she said. "I'll do any work around the barn if you'll teach me."

"It isn't easy, learning horses," Mr. Stolz told her. "Jeremy was in a saddle practically before he could walk."

"It doesn't have to be easy," Sky argued. "It just has to be horses. I don't care how much work it is."

Mr. Stolz looked at her keenly, and then nodded. "I don't have a lot of time myself, but if Jeremy will fill in, maybe we can get you on a horse. Hey, Jeremy!" He turned back into the ring, waited until Jeremy had finished the routine, and then approached his son.

Sky fixed her eyes on them, straining to hear what they were saying. Jeremy glanced at her once, a frown on his face, and then he shrugged. Mr. Stolz gave Sky a thumbs-up as his son wheeled the horse around and trotted toward the barn. Sky ran forward and swung the gate open as he reached it.

Behind her, she could hear Moose rumbling a half-hearted growl. Still holding the gate open, she glanced back. Moose was blocking the path of Athena who, even though she was holding her camera ready to shoot, appeared frozen in fear.

"Hi there," she squeaked, managing to wave a couple of fingers at Sky. "Any chance of calling off your dog...or hasn't he had lunch yet?"

Sky and Jeremy both pealed out laughter at the same time. Even Molly snorted and twitched her ears. Mr. Stolz shook his head in amusement and headed up to the house, while Athena smiled hopefully at them.

"Moose, behave yourself," Sky ordered as she swung the gate shut behind Jeremy and Molly. The dog grunted and lay down, clearly reluctant to give up the game of scaring Athena into rabbity panic.

"Don't you hate to see a dog sulk," Athena said.

Moose *woofed* and she leapt backwards, climbing up a rung of the fence. Moose relaxed again, thin black lips pulled into a smirk. A bit of drool slipped down from his sharp white teeth. He grunted in his throat and sank back into the grass, panting gently.

"Okay," Athena said. "Just kidding, right?" But she climbed down and, at a very safe distance, followed Sky, Jeremy, and Molly into the barn.

While the two girls watched, Jeremy slipped off the mare's bridle, replacing it with a halter and lead rope that he tied to a ring set in the wall. Next, he unbuckled the smooth English saddle, pulled it off Molly's back and heaved it into Sky's arms. He grinned when she nearly collapsed under the sudden weight.

"It goes over there." He gestured toward an open room containing bridles, saddles, and other horse tack. Sky hauled the saddle over, and at his nod, placed it squarely on a waiting rack. In the background, she could hear the soft clicks of Athena's camera and the contented stamps, whickers and munches as Molly dug into a feed bag that Jeremy had slid over her nose.

"First lesson," Jeremy called as he set his hard hat on a shelf. "Bring over the brushes."

Sky picked up a box of grooming implements and fingered them, feeling the smooth, slightly greasy sheen of the well-used combs. Breathing in deeply, she savored the scents of hay, leather, and horse that floated everywhere in the barn.

"You start like this," Jeremy said taking one of the brushes and sliding it over Molly's shoulder. "Nice, smooth motions."

Sky picked up her own brush and with one hand on Molly's neck, her fingers feeling the muscles and pulsing blood under the mare's velvety coat, began a slow, sure sweep of over the horse's shoulder. Athena snapped pictures, Jeremy paused only to check that the skinny kid was grooming his beloved mare correctly, and Sky without a pause in her work, let out a sigh of contentment unexpectedly found. She could do this. She could feel surety stirring in her blood...*horse magic.*

"So, how come you're staying at Judy Whitmore's?" Athena interrupted Sky's dreams.

"She's my great-aunt," Sky said. "I'm staying while my mom looks for work."

"Who's your mother?" Jeremy ducked under Molly's neck and frowned at her.

"Probably Judy's niece," Athena offered. Both Jeremy and Sky glared at her. Athena laughed and ambled to the far side of the barn, trying out different angles and settings as she shot photos of patterns of light and shadow woven across the walls and stalls.

"Funny," Jeremy growled. "I mean it, Sky. Who is your mom?"

Sky flushed, feeling trapped by his insistence. "Her name's Lindey. Why do you care?"

Jeremy stared. "My mom was her older sister," he muttered. "Seems we're cousins."

Sky felt as if the horse had just hoofed her in the stomach. Her mom had talked about how her own parents had died when she was fourteen, and that she'd been all alone except for her Aunt Judy. Had she ever mentioned an older sister?

"Mom never said anything about a sister..." she trailed off and returned to grooming Molly, letting the slow sweep of the brush calm her seething emotions. More of her mom's secrets.

"My mom, Marie, was twelve years older and I don't think they got along. Then Lindey took off." His voice hardened. "We didn't even know where to find her when my mom died."

Sky pressed her forehead against Molly's warm neck and held her breath to force back the emotions flooding her. Anger. Always anger. She breathed deeply, willing the warmth of the horses to push the bitterness away, to let herself be happy just for a few moments.

Jeremy returned to his side of Molly, and although his head was higher than Molly's back, quietly combed her sides and flanks without looking at Sky. He spoke slowly, his voice so quiet, it murmured in Sky's ears like a memory. "When your dad wiped out on his motorcycle and Lindey took off, Mom used to worry about her and her baby. About you. She was like that," he said slowly. "She used to worry about people. She didn't know you, but she worried about you. Worried whether Lindey was looking after you right. Wanted her to come home with you. But the one time Mom found her, Lindey wouldn't come."

Sky looked at him over Molly's back. "What happened to your mom?" she whispered.

Jeremy's hands smoothed Molly's mane. "Breast cancer," he said. "They didn't catch it soon enough. She died last fall."

Impulsively, Sky reached her fingers toward him. "I'm sorry, Jeremy."

He nodded. "Yeah. The next thing I should show you is how to clean her hooves...." Patting Molly's shoulder, he reached for the picks.

"Did you see this?" Athena suddenly called. "Jeremy, you've got the all-time champion spider web over here by the window. And that big fat spider could about eat one of your horses!" A flurry of clicks emanated from the corner.

Jeremy rolled his eyes and when his lips twitched upwards, Sky somehow couldn't help but smile back – at the cousin she'd never known she had.

Chapter 12

Sky worked with Jeremy for two hours cleaning tack and mucking out stalls. He insisted that every aspect of the care of his horses be perfect. Sky didn't mind. He didn't say much beyond telling her to redo work that wasn't exactly to his standards, but he was gentle with the horses, and surprisingly patient with her.

Athena shot a few more pictures and announced that she was going to work on them for yet another big contest. When she received no reaction, she sidled past Moose and disappeared. Sky didn't care. Her whole attention lay in sucking in every bit of knowledge and skill she could absorb. The work was hard and smelly, but even as a strand of sticky hair flopped over her sweating face, Sky smiled inside. Jeremy kept his eyes on her critically but other than grunting directions, made few comments.

As she led Molly back to the pasture, the sound of *clip-clopping* hooves and the sudden snorts of hot breath as the horse blew into her shoulder, thrilled Sky to the core of her being. Unsnapping the lead rope, she set the mare loose to graze and wander. When the rest of the barn chores were done, Jeremy and she leaned companionably against the fence.

"So, you want to go for a ride?" Jeremy asked lazily.

Sky twisted to look at him. Was this a tease?

"Just a short ride," he said over his shoulder as he walked toward the gate. "I told my dad I'd done all my homework, but that wasn't the whole truth. I have a big project to turn in when spring break is over."

"Sure...I guess." It was all Sky could do to not pump the air. She was going to get on a horse. It was happening. The old magic or whatever was like a stream sweeping her toward horses...toward the white horse.

"Idiot," she muttered under her breath. "Stupid, Sky. It's just a horse. People ride them all the time."

But she didn't. She never had before...

She followed Jeremy into the field and, with a couple of clicks of his tongue, he called Prince Caspian and Firefly. Holding their manes, Jeremy led them into the barn, where he showed Sky how to put on the horses' saddles and bridles so that they were tight enough but did not make their mounts uncomfortable. Jeremy fitted her with a pair of old riding boots and a hard hat, boosted her up onto Firefly's back, and then mounted Prince Caspian himself.

"Hold the reins like this," he demonstrated. "And sit straight like I am. Eyes up. Heels down. The horse goes where you look. We'll take it nice and easy at first."

The horses pranced a little, and Sky found herself swaying into the motion of Firefly, her taut gymnast's muscles compensating for the horse's movement as they left the barn.

"This way," Jeremy said. Prince Caspian leapt into a trot, following a dirt lane that wound behind the house and into a thick stand of trees. In reckless joy, Sky urged Firefly to follow, and ignoring the surprising amount of bouncing, leaned forward to take the path.

"*Gee-up*," Sky called out and the horse responded.

Firefly's smooth muscles stretched and swelled as they trotted and then galloped down the lane. Jeremy looked back, saw them gaining and with a whoop, kicked Prince Caspian into a gallop. Sky leaned forward until Firefly's mane slapped her cheeks, stinging, and making her eyes squint. They flew past the trees, pounding the ground, swishing with the wind. Above, the branches blurred into a green canopy. Sky laughed aloud – she had never been so alive.

Horses. She felt herself blending with the smell, the speed, the warm life of her horse.

Smiling, Jeremy signaled her to slow down. "Don't want you to fall your first time out."

As they made their way along the trail, he carefully demonstrating more of the skills she needed. Before long, he led them past the woods, across a field and then down a slope to a trail beside the caramel brown Snohomish River. Then laughing, breathing hard, they reined in for a moment to gaze across the wide floodplain, emerald green with lush spring plants, dotted with lazy black cattle. The grey geometric towers of the nearby city of Everett formed a backdrop to the green fields.

"Thought you said you hadn't ridden before?" Jeremy said.

"I haven't," Sky replied. "Except I feel like I have. Always."

Jeremy shrugged. "Then you're a natural."

Heat simmering in her face at his laconic praise, Sky guided her horse beside Prince Caspian as they walked alongside the river.

"You can see the mountain past those trees." Jeremy pointed to a dense wood crowding the riverbank a hundred yards farther along. Prince Caspian cantered forward again, with

Firefly trotting briskly behind. The path led through the trees, but once they emerged on the other side, Sky saw the brilliant white mass of Mount Rainier dominating the southern horizon. They pulled up the horses to stand side by side.

"My mom and I used to ride down here a lot," Jeremy said. "It was a game, to see if the mountain was out."

Sky looked at him, puzzled.

"It's a volcano, not like most of the other mountains around. It's huge," Jeremy explained, "and so it's hard to tell how far away it is. If the weather is hazy or rainy, it's shrouded and disappears. When you can see it, we say the mountain is out." He flushed a little. "Dumb, I guess, but it was a joke I had with my mom."

He wheeled his horse around then, and without saying anything headed back the way they had come. Sky stared out at the conical mountain a moment longer and then followed him. Had her mom and dad had grown up looking to see if the mountain was out? Sky clenched her teeth and urged Firefly forward, hanging on grimly, making the return to the barn a race. Jeremy won, but only by a few steps – and he'd had a head start.

*   *   *

"Dinner, honey!" Athena's mom called up the stairs.

Athena grimaced. A week into her mom's *Return of the Devoted Parent* extravaganza and already she was longing for the days of frozen meals zapped in the microwave. Last night they had eaten Avocado-Tofu-Asian-Surprise casserole. She had always liked avocados before and strongly suspected if anyone in Asia knew that that meal had been blamed on them, there would be serious diplomatic repercussions.

Today, her mom had promised a "divinely wonderful New York salad." Athena and her dad had forced smiles, but their eyes had met over the table with a look of mutual suffering.

"Athena?"

"I'm coming!" Athena yelled in the general direction of the staircase.

Almost done.

With a click, the photo was on its way, entered in the national contest, just minutes before the final deadline. She had called it *Sky Whitmore flying*. And if she did say so herself, it was magnificent. The shot was unbelievable – that weird kid Sky mid-air above the fence in some kind of gymnastics flip with Neil's crazy stallion rearing in the stormy background like something out of a myth. It was so supernaturally clear that even the barn's painted sign, *McClelland Stables*, could be made out in the corner. And the photo was so awesomely, incredibly amazing, it sent shivers along Athena's spine.

With a sigh of satisfaction, she headed for the stairs just as another impatient "*Athena!*" rose from below. Just wait until she won this contest. Her mother wouldn't be the only famous photographer!

*   *   *

As Sky floated into the house in a beautiful horse-filled dream, Aunt Judy looked up from the table where she was reading a newspaper. A crumb-covered plate sat empty before her.

"Good of you to show up for dinner," Aunt Judy remarked.

Sky thudded down from the joyful clouds as sudden rage surged over her. She stood motionless, carefully expressionless, poised to escape if Aunt Judy's anger threatened to flood over her. As Moose plunked himself on the carpet, panting, her great-aunt rose from the table, gathering up the dishes.

"This isn't a restaurant," she said sharply. "I want you here at mealtime and I want to know where you have gone when it isn't mealtime. I didn't know where to find you. That irritates me and being irritated makes me even more irritated." She shot a look at Sky. "Don't you even have the manners to apologize?"

"Sorry," Sky said, her voice flat. Moose looked worriedly from one to the other, his big head swinging between them like he was watching a tennis match.

"You'd be well served to miss dinner altogether," Aunt Judy grumbled. "There's a plate of turkey and potatoes for you in the oven. And cauliflower. If you don't like cauliflower you're out of luck."

Sky swallowed. "Thank you, Aunt Judy. And I'm sorry I was late."

Her great-aunt frowned, pushed at Moose with her foot, and snapped, "Will you get out of my way, you overgrown horse!" When the dog looked up in confusion, she sighed, stepped over him and went into the kitchen to deposit the dishes on the drainboard. "Dinner is at six," she told Sky. "If the schedule gets off, Moose gets grumpy."

With a lot of clattering, her aunt filled Moose's dish with dried food, poured some gravy over it, and set it on the floor. When Moose dove in, she took a plate covered in aluminum foil from the oven and set it on the stovetop.

"You're too skinny to miss meals," Aunt Judy commented.

"Sorry I was late," Sky repeated.

"No harm done, except to my temper, which is never great anyway. I've unfortunately got more work I have to do tonight. I'm never going to make this deadline," she grumbled and headed back upstairs to her office.

Sky forced her paralyzed legs to move, took a deep breath, rolled the stiff muscles in her shoulders and then with a sharp lurch of relief, took her dinner to the table. His own bowl emptied, Moose padded after her, gazing up with starvation-dimmed eyes as she unwrapped the meal.

It was a really big plate. Her shoulders relaxed more as she realized that at least Aunt Judy was generous with food. Sky ate about half of it. The rest she divided – one quarter into Moose's mouth and one quarter carefully rewrapped in foil.

"It'll be good for a day or two, maybe," she murmured to Moose, and then wondered in hot anxiety whether she really needed to keep stashing food. But Aunt Judy had impatiently threatened to have her do without meals for being late or making her angry. Probably she didn't mean it. Probably it would never happen. But Sky couldn't risk that desperate hunger again, couldn't take the chance of anything weakening her. If her mom's plans fell apart...if the Nightmare found her...

Sky's breath came in hard gasps that hurt her chest. And the white horse...she had to save him, too.

She ran up the stairs and slid the packet in behind another book. Then hesitating a little, she went and stood at the door to Aunt Judy's office. Her great-aunt was rapidly typing an email. Sky coughed a little to get her aunt's attention.

Startled, Aunt Judy twisted around.

"I'm...um...going outside for a bit," Sky said.

"Thank you for telling me," Aunt Judy said. "Don't get lost when the sun goes down. No streetlights around here and it's easy to lose your bearings."

"I'll watch out," Sky said, "and...um...don't worry about me."

"Works for me," Aunt Judy muttered, swiveling around in her chair, and starting on her keyboard again. Sky backed up, almost tripped over Moose, and then hurried down the stairs.

Now that she knew the path to the white horse's paddock, Sky ran toward it. The sun slanted across the green leaves and the shadows were lengthening, but she judged she had a little more than an hour of daylight left. Excitement made her almost breathless. The white stallion would respond to her. Just to her. Jeremy had said she was a natural, but most of all, she was aware of a swirling in her blood. An inherited memory awakening. A memory of something...maybe magic...she thought with a shiver. Maybe magic encoded in her DNA.

Chapter 13

Moose loped beside Sky, long tongue flapping, past the tangle of brambles and down the overgrown path leading to the white horse's enclosure. Sky broke from the trees, ladder-climbed the board fence and with careful confidence, balanced on the top board to gaze out toward the stallion. He stood in the center of the field, blowing a little, stamping his front hoof.

She was alone with the horse, with only Moose as their witness.

For sheer joy, relishing the regrowth of her strength, Sky did a slow back flip along the fence and then smoothly jumped down into the field. The horse watched her, almost motionless but for the slow swish of his elegant tail and the lift and flutter of his white mane in the breeze. Digging an apple liberated from Aunt Judy's fridge out of her pocket, Sky moved slowly toward the animal, arm outstretched, fruit on her upturned palm. The stallion's ears twitched forward and back; he danced on his hooves, the strong muscles in his shoulders quivering. With desperate concentration, Sky calmed her breathing and kept her steps to a measured pace that held no menace. She turned her eyes slightly downward so the horse wouldn't interpret her stare as a challenge.

"Hey," she said in a soft monotone. "It's okay. I know the kinds of things they've done to you. They've done them to me too – so I get it. But we're strong. We've survived it all. And we're going to be friends. We'll be stronger than all of them."

The horse pranced to one side and then the other, half skittish, half playful. Sky stopped, waiting motionlessly, arm still outstretched. Knowing how lingering fear could cloud every reaction and feeling – for an animal as well as herself – she resumed talking slowly and gently. In time, the horse would know her voice, would know she was safe no matter what the rest of the world tried to do.

When he knew that, he would come to her. Knowing fear the way she did, Sky would wait for that moment. Trust that the moment would come.

"I've brought an apple for you," she spoke in the same soft lilt. "I'll bring you something every day. Paying it forward until you know I'm okay."

The horse was stretching his head out toward her; his feet were beginning to step in her direction when Moose suddenly leapt to his feet and barked. Sky froze. The horse spun on its hooves and tore to the far side of the pasture.

"*Hey!*" Neil shouted. "*You, get out of there!*"

A split second of frozen panic, and then, dropping the apple, Sky sprinted for the fence. On the far side, Moose barked wildly, slamming his giant paws against the boards so that she almost lost her balance as she vaulted over. Without pausing, Sky dove into the shelter of the shadowed trees.

Was Neil following her? What would he do if he caught her? Panic tore through her. She ran – scratching herself on undergrowth, scrambling over fallen trees.

She'd heard that kind of angry boom in the Nightmare's voice – and when he'd caught her...

If he caught her...Sky dodged between trunks, wrenched away from snagging branches, frantic for a place to hide...finally curled up like a wounded animal, she pressed into a half-hollow tree trunk.

Rain pattered lightly on the highest leaves, but few drops reached the ground where Sky huddled, body wracked with the shuddering sobs she tried to hold back. Moose pushed at her with his big head, whining, pawing awkwardly at her knee.

Sky was barely aware of him, hardly conscious of anything beyond the terrible thudding of her heart, the gasping air that didn't seem to quite fill her lungs, and the scene playing over and over again across her mind. The horror memories, all stabbing pain and flashbulb stills.

Ten-year-old Sky has wandered into the Nightmare's empty home office. She is impressed with the thick brown carpet and the dark wood panel, all smelling like his expensive cigars. With a delighted smile she sits at his desk, swiveling his big leather chair a little while she examines the rows of numbers on his laptop screen.

He strides into the room and she smiles at him, but his eyes are icy cold. Silently he snaps the laptop closed, and then grips her shoulder with fingers like a steel claw, dragging her out of the chair, across the room and into the hall. She cries out and struggles, but he slaps her.

For a second or two she is stunned into silence, but then rage consumes her. "Mommy!" Sky screams, but no one else is there so she kicks him in the leg. The Nightmare slams her against the wall. Air whooshes from her lungs and she can't breathe. Her shoulder screams in pain. Her arm dangles numbly. She stares up in confusion and terror as he stands over her.

There is no flush of anger on his handsome face, but his eyes are the color of old frost that forms over murky puddles. Thoughtfully, the Nightmare takes out one of his expensive cigars, and with a flick of his gold lighter, lights it. He puffs a few times and then inhales deeply.

With pursed lips, he blows out a snaking curl of smoke, all the while staring down at her with his ice-chip eyes. Silence stretches between them. Sky hears only her own soft, panting breaths. Then he again snaps alive a blue-orange flame. Slowly, he brings the flame closer and closer to her cheek, moving it like a tiny dancer twirling sinuously toward her. The heat sears her skin and Sky screams. She struggles to run, but The Nightmare's manicured hand, twists her shoulder.

Sky squeezes her eyes closed and clenches her teeth over the screams. Distantly, she hears the sound of the door from the garage into the kitchen opening. She opens her eyes as a breath of cool air across her cheek causes the flame to waver.

"I'm home," her mother calls.

"You ugly little brat," the Nightmare says softly, pleasantly, "don't you ever set foot in my office again."

Sky shakes her head frantically and stares at the flame just beyond the tip of her nose. Never again. Never again.

"And don't you mention this to your stupid mother either," he whispers, "or I'll really hurt you – and her too. Really."

He smiles, flicks the lighter a of couple times, and strolls back into his office, humming under his breath. Through the open door, Sky sees him sit in his leather office chair, open the laptop, and begin typing, not even glancing back at her.

Sky leans against the wall, her shoulder throbbing. In the kitchen, her mom opens and shuts cupboards, putting away the groceries. Over

*the kitchen noises, Sky hears a thin
mewling sound. Dizzily, she realizes
that those terrible sounds are coming
from her half-open mouth.*

*Her mom calls from the other side
of the house. "Want some hot chocolate?"*

*Sky slowly, painfully thrusts herself
upright and, cradling her arm, stumbles
toward her pretty, new bedroom. "No
thanks," she replies with almost no
wobble to her voice.*

*Her mother can never know, or
the Nightmare will...*

*Her mother never knows. She never
knows. Sky keeps her mom safe and
never breathes a word.*

Gradually, Sky became aware of the woods
around her as the flash memory receded and
became just a memory again. Angrily she
scrubbed her face with her fists, forcing the
thin screams back into her throat, until the
only noises rising above the chittering birds
and swishing leaves were Moose's anxious
whines and doggy murmurs. Her heart still
pounded, and she swallowed hard as she used
the tree to push herself upright again.

She clenched her fists. How could she have
been sucked back into that horrific memory?
Couldn't she just forget those days? They were

done. They were gone. There was no flame blistering her cheek or steel fingers crushing her shoulder. She wasn't ten anymore. And she had learned to beat the Nightmare. She'd cached countless stores of food, made her body strong and fast, and stolen the thumb drive full of his secrets.

And she and her mom had escaped the monster at last.

Escape.

But now Neil had nearly caught her. The memory of trespassing in the Nightmare's office rewound in her mind and began to replay... *he brings the flame closer and closer to her cheek, moving it like a tiny dancer...* Moose bunted her chest and Sky moaned, but the rewind was broken for now. She grabbed the dog's big head and buried her face in his fur, drawing a great shuddering breath.

"He won't scare me away. I'm not afraid of Neil and I'm not afraid of the Nightmare!" she muttered into the warm fur. A huge, pathetic lie declared over a thudding heart. But Moose wagged his tail and sloshed his tongue adoringly over her neck. He believed her.

Taking deep breaths, Sky forced herself to stop shaking. She was okay now. And she was going to stay okay because her mom had caught on, finally. The two of them had worked together to escape. The Nightmare would never find them. Sky would never see him again.

Neil wasn't like the Nightmare and besides, Moose would protect her, Sky thought wildly. Just like she was going to protect the white stallion. Someone had starved and tormented him, just like the Nightmare had starved and tormented her. But she would protect the horse just as she had protected her mother and herself. The memories festering in her head would not take over her life. She was okay. If she had to lie to Aunt Judy and Neil about the horse, she would. She would be ready.

The Nightmare would never win again. Never.

Determined, Sky stilled her trembling limbs and slipped back to the white stallion's paddock. Standing motionless in the shadow of the trees, she watched Neil try to put a halter on the horse and then once again, catapult over the fence when the horse charged him. Sky rejoiced at the horse's spirit and at the knowledge that until Neil had startled him, the magnificent creature had been willing to approach her.

"He'll let me ride him," Sky whispered to Moose. "He knows he can trust me. Just you wait, Moose. He's going to be my horse."

Sky stared a while longer. With Neil and the stablemen around, it was too dangerous to approach the horse during the day. But at night the stallion would be alone. When the world slept, she would become his friend, partner, and protector. In the moonlight, the horse magic in her soul would rise and Sky knew now that she would answer its call. She would sit astride the white stallion's broad back and cling to his shining mane. And no one would know. No one.

Sky, the horse, and the dog would be invincible. She was sure of it.

"Tonight," she told Moose. "We'll start tonight."

Chapter 14

Jeremy was riding again – really riding. He had kept the horses exercised when his mom was ill and after she'd died, but he hadn't had the heart to ride alone. Before then, it had always been the two of them training and competing. His dad was an amazing trainer of both horses and riders, but mostly he'd been on the sidelines advising and teaching. Mike obsessed over the team sports at school, and so Jeremy and his mom had shared the equestrian adventure. He knew it was stupid, but for months it had seemed like he was betraying his mom by training without her.

But with the spring air and the glorious feeling of his champion horses, he felt like she was at his shoulder whispering encouragement and cheering him on. Maybe she was glad too, that her sister's kid had joined them. Stupid, but Jeremy couldn't shake the belief that it somehow pleased his mom.

Riding Molly around the training ring, Jeremy watched for Sky. She wasn't really ready to train with him, but he recognized that fierce love of horses and the fight to win that he and his mom had shared. His dad had liked working with them, but he loved his job at the regional utilities company. His success there paid for Jeremy and his mom's passion for competition.

And there was that girl now, silent as a ghost, standing by the fence with Moose beside her. With a flash of irritation, Jeremy saw that once again his horses were ambling toward her, practically frisking in greeting. No way he was jealous...but what was that all about?

He finished his session with Molly, completely ignoring his newfound cousin. But when he turned toward the barn, the horses had drifted to this end of the pasture and she had the gate pulled open. He grunted thanks and trotted into the barn. Sky whisked in behind him and was ready with the brushes before he had even swung down from Molly's back. For several minutes they worked without speaking. While Jeremy carefully combed knots from his mare's mane, Sky picked up a broom and began sweeping the cement floor. The *swish, swish* suddenly spooked Molly and she tossed her head nervously. Jeremy grabbed her halter strap and murmured reassuringly to her. The horse snorted and stamped her rear hoof a couple of times, then let him lead her into her stall. With the gate shut behind her, she began nosing the oats in her feed trough.

Sky watched with interest. "What do you do if your horse acts all wild?"

Jeremy shrugged. "Our horses don't act wild. We mostly raise and train them ourselves." He rolled his shoulders, loosening the muscles that obviously needed more of a workout than he'd been giving them.

"You raised all of them?" Sky's brow furrowed. "Were they born here?"

"Dad buys them when they're young, before anyone's started their training." Jeremy heaved the saddle back to the tack room. "Although Firefly was a bit of a mess. The people didn't know how to train and confused her. That took a while to get her taught right."

"But what do you *do*?" Sky insisted.

Jeremy frowned. "Well, you start off getting them to trust you. Then you get them used to the bridle, then the saddle and training bits. You know, start off easy. Keep everything consistent and make sure the horse works ahead in small steps, so it gets it right and trusts the rider to steer it in the right way...I don't know," he said helplessly. "We just do it. You can watch and see."

Over the days, Sky watched and somehow managed to see – the combination of gentleness and firmness, the no-nonsense insistence that the horse obey a command and the clear, tiny steps of pacing and exact movement. Rewards, lavish pride, and Jeremy's belief that his horses could do anything better than any other horse.

As Sky watched, held reins, groomed, cleaned tack and received lessons from her new cousin and uncle on how to sit properly, flow with the horse's movements and with the lightest pressure, direct those great, glorious animals into walks, trots, canters and finally jumps and dances. The horses, especially Firefly, would turn their heads back, roll their huge brown eyes and snort in indulgent laughs at her ineptitude. Sky learned from Jeremy and most of all she learned from the horses. She loved the feel of their powerful muscles tightening and stretching as they sailed over a jump, the blowing snorts of their horsey amusement, the jangle of tack and the wind blowing over her face as they thundered across the courses and trails.

She had found heaven.

Athena documented every step, dodging Moose, chortling over camera shots, running for the fence any time one of the horses ambled her way, and filling the air with her monologues of directions, exclamations, and chirpy shrieks. Before long, Jeremy and Sky completely ignored her presence.

Jeremy's dad would join them as soon as he'd changed from his daytime suit and tie, into jeans and a stained sweatshirt. Then their lessons became formal and exacting.

"Thinking about competing in the state fair?" he asked Jeremy Thursday evening as the three of them bedded the horses down for the night and Athena dodged around like a storm-driven fly.

"Maybe," Jeremy shrugged.

Sky looked from one to the other as they avoided looking at each other.

"Last year for the junior category," her uncle went on, pausing to work a knot out of Prince Caspian's mane. "Give you a chance to get used to competition again. And Molly ought to have a shot at being a champion. Your mom had her almost ready. Wouldn't hurt us financially either to get some prize money or breeding fees."

"I'll think about it," Jeremy said.

"That's all I ask," his dad replied. His eyes swung over to Athena who was standing with her camera tipped at an angle resembling a broken jack-in-the box. "That should be quite a photo. Making an album?" He raised an eyebrow.

"An album? You aren't the only people who compete," Athena said with frosty dignity. "I call this series, '*Dream Builders*'!" A slight, hopeful smile tweaked up the corners of her mouth and her eyes darted across their faces, waiting for a flicker of enthusiasm. Nothing. She sighed. "Philistines. I am building a portfolio of photos for sale online. And I enter contests, Mr. Stolz. Cash prizes, sometimes. New equipment, sometimes. Recognition... priceless...and not much available."

Mr. Stolz ran a thoughtful hand over Prince Caspian's flank. "The horses look good in these photos?" At his nod, Sky gave a tug on the horse's halter and led him toward his stall, right where Athena was standing.

The girl was so focused on her camera prowess, that she didn't register the proximity of the horse. "When I take pictures, your horses look like champions. And I am also an expert at photoshopping. Why, I submitted the most amazing photo last week..."

At that, Prince Caspian stamped a hoof and snorted. Athena shrieked and spider crawled up a stack of hay bales.

"Horses may not be my best subject," she announced with a slightly glazed smile. Sky laughed and her uncle forced back a smile.

"I might be interested in buying a few of the photos," he said.

"You are?" Athena scuttled back down the hay bales. "You are...?" she repeated.

"Don't go spooking the horses," Jeremy ordered without letting a smile creep over his face.

Sky came out of the stall, pushed the door shut, and latched it. "All safe," she told Athena. She grinned across at Jeremy when their friend smiled brightly and visibly relaxed.

"I need some good shots," Mr. Stolz told them. "A fellow got hold of Neil McClelland this morning, offering him a sweet deal to get into a breeding consortium. He wants $10,000 to buy in. Once I hear what he has to say, I'll either invest or set up my own program. We have champion quality horses here. But I'll need some good photos and videos of our animals."

"Then I'm your woman," Athena declared. "Let me know what you want, and I'll deliver. We can talk about price when you see the work I do."

Mr. Stolz rubbed his chin and nodded. "Sounds good. It's time Jeremy and I started working on the dream he and his mom had. We'll start with pictures, but we're sure going to need some cash. It always comes down to the money."

Susan Brown

Chapter 15

The days working the horses exhausted Sky like the fiercest gymnastics competitions. But unlike those, she tackled the endless chores with throbbing eagerness.

But the nights...they were the stuff of magic.

Each night, Sky lay under a quilt, bedside alarm set on low volume. Judy usually packed her work in, watched the news, and retired – giving Sky a handful of hours to sleep. When the alarm rang softly, just past midnight, Sky silently slid from between the covers and pulled on her clothes. Moose would watch in puzzled silence, but then padded down the stairs after her.

She had her routine: check that the downstairs bathroom window was open – a survival trick to always have a way to get in or out; put a carrot or apple into her pocket; silently slide back the deadbolt. Then with Moose following, ease into the night.

For Sky, this dark world held all the fear and lure of an enchantment. Familiar shapes stretched and distorted. Muffled sounds reverberated in the shadows. Jagged screams echoed from hunters and hunted. Leaves rustled in fitful breezes. Stars shone down in shards of light. The moon drifted in and out of clouds.

Sky moved carefully, keeping to the velvety dark beside bushes and under trees. The only sound of their passing was Moose's soft panting. As another despairing cry tore the night, she clenched her jaw against the rush of pity for the deaths of those small creatures. The Nightmare always bragged that he was a hunter, savoring his victories, never wasting a thought for those he destroyed. Sky hated him with her every breath and heartbeat. He didn't hunt like the hawks and coyotes and eagles. He hunted like a weasel, full of blood lust and cruelty. And even a weasel was driven by harsh instinct, not sadistic greed, Sky thought.

She shook her head to clear those crippling ideas, moving swiftly along the narrow path to the pasture. With a long sigh, as she saw the white stallion standing in the center of the field, moonlight pooling across his head, mane, and back like a halo. He whickered and tossed his head at the sight of her, making the moonglow shimmer outward.

"I'm here," Sky breathed. Stupid thing to say. He could see her.

She leaned against the fence and stood a moment looking toward the barns, arena, and distant house. All dark but for a couple of muted lights by the barn doors. While those horsemen slept, she would form a bond of trust with the horse – her horse.

Sky vaulted into the paddock and walked slowly, swaying in the rhythm of night. Once again, she held out her hand with an apple lying on her flattened palm. The horse whickered again, a sound like a soft laugh. But he didn't move, simply waited for Sky to come to him.

"You could be like some kind of Pegasus," Sky murmured as the bristly softness of his lips brushed her skin. In two quick bites, the apple was gone. The horse stood blinking, blowing a little, as her hand slid over his nose. Sky felt the warmth of his face, the soft shush of blood beneath his skin, an echo of his great heart.

She laid her forehead against his cheek, aware that he was a wild horse, that she who guarded herself against every danger was risking her life. But she knew in every way possible, that if the stallion was wild and untamed, he was also good. That he would know she came to him with an open heart and that alone made her safe in his company.

The thought drifted across her mind that after all the time she had spent with Jeremy's horses, she knew that the white stallion was different. For all their liveliness and idiosyncrasies, the other horses did not radiate the same wildness as this creature.

"So maybe not Pegasus," Sky whispered into his neck. "How about the unicorn that comes to the Whitmore women when they're in trouble?"

The stallion neighed softly and bunted her shoulder.

Sky smiled. "I wish. Mom and I have so much trouble...so much."

For an instant the memory of the Nightmare oozed into the perfect night. The stallion stamped his hoof and tossed his head.

"You're right." Fingers entwined in the horse's mane, Sky whispered, "Any chance you'll let me on your back? I'll bring you more treats."

The horse huffed a little, but when Sky pulled slightly, he came with her to the fence. The stallion dipped his head over the fence to briefly touch noses with Moose, then stood unmoving. He twisted his head to watch as Sky climbed the boards and then slid awkwardly onto his broad back.

"This is frigging amazing," she whispered.

Her legs straddled his back as he watched

her in amused curiosity. The stretch and grip in her legs had nothing to do with the muscles she'd built in gymnastics, but the last few days with Jeremy had helped.

Sky buried her fingers deep in the horse's mane, loving the warm scent rising from it, and the shimmering moonlight skittering across them. The whole night seemed draped in dark velvet – except for this one magical pool of brilliance.

"So...will you walk on?"

The horse flicked his ears but didn't move.

"Come on," Sky urged, lightly touching his sides with her heels. "Aren't we going to ride at all?"

The horse flicked his ears again, and seeming to snort with laughter, suddenly leapt and twisted. Caught off guard, Sky tumbled back over his haunches and down onto the muddy grass.

She lay there panting, grateful the ground was softer than any gym mat. The stallion ambled back and lowered his head to nibble on her hair.

"You did that on purpose." Sky wondered if she should stand up and try again or just lie there on the cool turf. The horse nudged her.

"All right," Sky muttered and slowly stood. She brushed the worst of the mud from her clothes, stretched her arms, back, and legs, and then rolled her shoulders. "Okay. One more time."

The stallion walked back to the fence and looked over at her, clearly waiting, inviting.

"So here goes nothing." Again, she climbed the fence and eased herself onto the horse's back. She felt the throb of his muscles beneath her hands as she slid them over his shoulders and once more wound her fingers into his mane.

"No dumping me this time," she warned the stallion. "Or you and me, finished. Got that?"

He looked back at her again, snorted, and then stepped forward. At first, he moved in a slow trot. Sky rose and fell, felt the muscles bunching and stretching in the horse's back. Felt her own muscles responding to the rhythm, to the magic of his elegant pace. His speed increased until they cantered around and around the pasture.

"Oh...wow," Sky managed, one hand stroking his neck. "I sure wish we could go for a real ride."

As if spurred on by her words, the horse abruptly picked up speed and galloped – straight at the fence.

She was going to die. The horse would crash into the fence, or buck and throw her over. She would break and die.

"No way," Sky hissed. "You won't get rid of me that easy!" In a flash, she crouched down, gripping his mane, and clapping her knees to his sides.

And then it happened. The stallion's muscles bunched; she felt his shoulders and hindquarters stretch as they sailed over the fence. Practically flew...as though it was just a dream.

The stallion galloped along the lane, moonlight streaming behind him. Sky held on, panting, exulting – alive as she had never been alive before. All wound into the magical glory of this horse. *Her* horse.

They hurtled on and on, down to the river where fog rose like smoke from the ground. The horse's hooves flashed in and out of the mist as though he galloped on air itself.

Flying, Sky thought. *We are flying*.

The moon glimmered on her and on the horse...and his silver horn shone in its light.

The magic has come alive, Sky rejoiced. She was part of the magic, part of the moonlight. Part of every story she had ever heard.

The magic is alive...

They galloped for what seemed like hours, like days, like all eternity. Through greening fields and shadowed woods, past tumbling rivers and rushing waterfalls, up rolling hills and craggy mountains. Her heart beat in time with the thudding hooves, and when the great white stallion bugled to the starry night sky, Sky cried out in joy. And then when she became so tired she didn't know if she could hold on any longer, she felt the horse drift downwards and they were back in his field. The stallion circled, slowed, and stood blowing and pawing the earth with one hoof.

Sky slid from his back and leaned against him, breathing in the scent of his horsey sweat mixed with morning breeze and fading magic. She gazed wonderingly up at the gleaming white head. There was no horn. Above them, the moon dimmed and slid behind a cloud. The birds began chirping and the air carried the tang of fresh dew. Dawn crept upward, a grey light in the eastern sky.

The horse wandered away from her and began cropping grass, his tail swishing lightly in the swelling light.

Moose stood up by the fence, watching her. He barked once, sharply, and Sky, though nearly too tired to move, scaled the fence, and with a last look back at the grazing white stallion, walked wearily home to the farmhouse.

She couldn't think. Couldn't understand.

But the door was still unlocked. Aunt Judy still snored softly in her room, and Sky with her own sigh of weariness slipped into bed. For now, she wouldn't even try to think or understand.

For now, she would drift into different dreams.

Tomorrow, she would understand, she thought drowsily. Tomorrow.

Chapter 16

"Guys!" Athena shrilled. "I did it! I won!"

Sky looked up from sweeping the old straw and mud into a pile on the cement floor. Her head ached and so did every other inch of her. Last night must have been a dream. What else could it have been? But her muscles felt more sore and stretched than she had ever experienced before, even after the most rigorous gymnastics sessions.

"Won what?" Jeremy asked with little interest. He rehung the tack he had been inspecting and cleaning.

"Well, actually I've not exactly won yet... but I will." Athena edged around Moose who gave only a perfunctory bark and dropped his head back on his paws. "I've been shortlisted for the national photo contest I entered. And now the public is voting!" She pulled a pen and folded paper from her pocket and waved it at Sky. "There's just one little formality." She smiled widely and flicked the paper open. "I need you to sign this release form. No biggie."

The world stopped. Sky struggled against the sudden pressure squeezing her chest. Her voice, coming from somewhere far away, asked hoarsely. "What release?"

"Well, really it's just a formality..." Athena faltered. "The photo I used is of you...I mean, I should have gotten the release right away," she continued in a rush. "But you were...um, sick. And I forgot. But don't worry – it's an amazing shot. You look great." She held out the paper again. "I have to scan this and send it in. Like right away."

"But...but the picture's not published yet?" Sky managed. Moose stood up, the fur on his spine ridging at the tension in her voice. Jeremy frowned and looked from one girl to the other.

Athena forced another smile and edged back from the dog. "Well, it's been published on the contest website as a finalist. But I'm pretty sure it will win. I mean how could it not?" Her eyes sparkled again. "It was the night of the storm, and you were doing that gymnastics thing on the fence...and...and the horse was rearing in the background...I gave you full credit..." Athena's voice wavered. "I know I should have gotten the release..."

Sky had a sense that the ceiling of the barn was twirling as she stared upward. A sob escaped from her throat and her legs didn't seem able to hold her up any longer. "He'll find me," she whispered. She sat on a bale of hay and dropped her head in her hands.

"Who," Jeremy asked. "Who will find you?"

Sky looked up at him mutely. There were no words now for the horror that engulfed her, for the memories that tsunamied across her mind. "He...I...it's the Nightmare..." she ground out.

"Nightmare?" Athena demanded. "What nightmare? I mean that was a really wild night and I'll bet you're still stressed...but it was real. I have the pictures. It wasn't a nightmare at all. And just think," she insisted, "you might become famous. My photos are that good. *I'm* that good."

Sky wrapped her arms around herself and began rocking, back and forth. She had to do something. She had to get away. Run away before he found her. Before it was too late.

"Really..." Athena began again.

"Shut up, Athena," Jeremy said savagely. He gentled his voice. "What is it Sky? What's wrong?"

"He...he'll find me..." she managed.

Athena shifted from one foot to the other in front of them, while Jeremy sat beside his cousin. Awkwardly, he put his arm around her shoulders. "Tell me." His voice was a low rumble that Sky somehow found reassuring.

How could she explain...the terror and pain? Especially the terror. There was no place to hide. The Nightmare would shroud her life with expensive clothes, fancy house, smiling and smiling and smiling. And cruelty she couldn't stop...couldn't predict...

Her head was spinning again. The Nightmare's weapon was fear. She had to fight that terror more than anything – or he would win...always win. Even now, he was oozing closer. Her fear was his doorway to her mind. Endless fear. The mewling whimpers of terror were rising in her throat. She had to stop. Had to get control of herself...or he would win.

"Let us help." Jeremy's voice carried reassurance.

"I still don't get it," Athena muttered.

Sky lifted her chin. Heat rushed to her face, but she pushed her sleeve up to her shoulder. "This," she shot out. "Get this."

Four round scars shone pink against her skin. The terrible reason her mother had finally agreed to run. "He stubbed out his cigar on me," she hissed. "He likes fire. Almost as much as he likes to hurt people. We got away, barely. But if...if he finds us..."

A harsh indrawn breath from Jeremy. An inarticulate stuttering sound from Athena.

The world spun again. Sky dropped her sleeve and put her head down, doggedly beating the nausea, the feeling that she was spinning out of existence.

"I didn't know..." Athena faltered. "Maybe he won't see it...I mean it's really big contest, but if he isn't into photography..."

"That's why they have rules about releases, Athena," Jeremy growled. "But you don't think about that stuff. Just your own stupid pictures."

"They aren't stupid," Athena protested angrily.

"Does anything show Sky's name or location on the photo?" Jeremy demanded.

Athena swallowed. Her voice became small and thin. "I put her name in the title..." she said. "I was trying to give her credit. And...and I think you can see the sign for McClelland's stable."

Sky got to her feet and walked unsteadily to the barn door to look again at the horses serenely cropping grass in the pasture. The beautiful horses. If the Nightmare found her, she would never be with the horses again. And the white horse who needed her...

"Maybe...maybe he won't find it?" Athena insisted. "The internet is really big...and maybe he doesn't care about photography..."

"He'll find me," Sky said dully. She turned back to face them. "I took something of his, so he'll hunt for me. He never gives up."

Jeremy stood and walked over to her, touching her arm. "We'll look after you. We won't let him find you. We…we can call the police."

Sky shook her head in despair. "He'll find a way around that. He always finds a way around. He lies and flashes his money and sounds like such a great guy that no one believes he's a monster until it's too late. It'll be too late." She looked around wildly. "I have to get away. I have to run away. He might already be here!"

"No…it'll be okay," Athena cried. "I mean, people can't do that…"

"Yes, they can," Sky said wearily. "He does it and he gets away with it. Nobody cares if everything looks good."

"Maybe you should stop being so stupid, Athena." Jeremy snapped. "A lot of bad things happen to people. But you're so busy hiding behind your stupid camera you never see it."

"I don't hide," Athena yelled back. "And I do something besides riding horses around in a circle and teaching them to dance! I'm showing life. Real life!"

"Yeah, well you sure showed this. What are you going to do to fix it?" Jeremy bellowed.

Sky was trying to make her brain move. Think what to do. Get herself out of the sludge of fear that paralyzed her while the other two carried on their futile argument. They didn't know. Couldn't know...

"Oh, shut up, Jeremy." Athena took a deep breath and looked mournfully at Sky. "I'll withdraw the photo, Sky. I mean, I'm brilliant and there's always next year, right? And really...why should he go after you, now?"

"It does seem like a lot of trouble," Jeremy said slowly. "Is it revenge?"

"Maybe," Sky said. She scrubbed her face with her hands. She had to think. "But I told you I took something of his. Something he'll want back."

"What?" Jeremy asked. "What did you take?"

"A thumb drive," Sky said dully. "He...he cons people and I think the flash drive has some of his files on it."

Jeremy whistled softly. "Can it prove anything about him?"

Sky shrugged. "I don't know. I saw it sticking out of his laptop and just took it. I thought I could use it to blackmail him to stay away or even give it into the police. I wasn't thinking straight. It was stupid."

"I'll bet if he's a con man the police already know about him," Athena said with a flare of excitement. "You tell the police and they'll be all over it. What's his name?"

"I...I don't know," Sky said.

"How can you not know?" Athena demanded. "You aren't making all this up, are you?"

Sky laughed as panic washed over her. "See! See how it always goes!"

Jeremy scowled at Athena. "Shut up, Athena. We believe you, Sky. But why don't you know his name?"

Sky pushed back her hair and slumped against the barn's wall. "Because he uses new identities all the time. Especially online. He builds fancy websites for companies that don't exist, and then he scams people. But they never really know who is doing it."

"What do you call him, besides the Nightmare?" Athena's asked.

Sky shrugged again. "He told my mom his name is Phil Marlowe, but I know he took that from a book. He likes mysteries. I heard him use a couple of other names too, and they were all from mysteries. I looked them up at school. But what difference does it make? No one ever believes me!" She tried to damp down the hysteria in her voice, get her brain back under control. The Nightmare would win if she lost control.

"We do believe you," Athena said hesitantly. "And we can do something. I know we must be able to do something because we do believe you." She sidled past Moose to awkwardly pat Sky's arm. "I'll go take down the photo. Right now. No matter how well the online voting is going..."

She didn't move fast, but she turned and started walking down the lane. Moose barked once.

"Put a lid on it, fuzzy-face!" they heard her mutter at the dog.

188   Susan Brown

Chapter 17

"We will do something," Jeremy persisted. "We'll protect you, Sky. After all, we're family now."

Sky tried to smile but she didn't seem to be able to move her face. She was shaking so hard, she wasn't sure she could stand up much longer.

Jeremy stared out at the horses ambling around the pasture. "We have to tell people," he said. "The guy is like a spider that hides in the shadows. We'll shine light on what he's doing. For a start, I'll tell my dad and you tell your Aunt Judy."

"They won't believe me," Sky said dully. "Nobody ever believes what he does until it's too late."

"We'll make them believe you," Jeremy insisted. "My dad is at the breeding consortium meeting but as soon as he gets back, we'll tell him the whole thing. And Judy will have to believe you, too. We can use the thumb drive to convince them if we have to." He paused. "And the scars you have. They're pretty convincing, Sky."

"I guess."

How could she explain that the Nightmare had turned even her injuries against her? With his mellifluous voice, he'd explained to counselors and doctors that Sky was depressed. Suicidal. That she practiced self-harm.

Bleakly, Sky looked again at the beautiful horses. She couldn't leave them. Even if she lost in the end, she would fight. The horses somehow had brought magic into her heart; she would not, could not, surrender that no matter what the Nightmare threatened.

Jeremy touched her arm. "Let's get the thumb drive and see what's on it."

Shepherded by her cousin, flanked by Moose, Sky summoned the strength to make her legs move. Her blind terror was being helped by Jeremy's solid bulk and Moose's drooling jaws. Insensibly cheered, she held onto a vision of herself courageously astride the white stallion while Jeremy held the Nightmare down and Moose chewed on his manicured hands.

Judy was not at the house, so while Jeremy waited, Sky went upstairs to get the thumb drive. She pulled out packets of food – packets she'd forgotten about in the brief security of living with Aunt Judy. With revulsion she saw that the food inside each bag had rotted and turned black with mold. One of the bag's seal had a broken and the interior crawled with grey maggots.

Why had she been so stupid? As if a stash of leftover food could protect her from the Nightmare's horrors? She'd be better off believing in the Whitmore women's unicorn...

The unicorn...

Sky's chin lifted suddenly. Hope shot through her. How could she have forgotten, especially in the shadow of the Nightmare's threat? For once, her mom had been right, but not the way she had thought. Sky had fought for and found the magic. The unicorn had chosen her. Surely its glorious goodness could somehow beat the Nightmare's evil.

"Sky, you okay?" Jeremy called up the stairs.

"Be right there!" she answered.

Somehow, she had awakened old magic... and friendship. Both unexpected. Both real.

A laugh of sheer relief bubbled at the back of Sky's throat. There was a chance. She had a chance...

Her courage rose again. She would be strong like all the women in her family. Her mother's great-grandmother, saving the unicorn. Her grandmother building this farm into a working stable. Aunt Judy, raising her nieces and taking Sky in. Even her mother, Sky realized, had sacrificed herself trying to save her baby's father and now she was trying to save her daughter the only way she knew how.

And of them all, only her mom's great-grandmother, and now Sky, had touched the unicorn.

Sky hesitated, one hand gripping the maggot-filled baggie, the other holding the thumb drive. She had to think. And she had to think it through, not just impulsively react the way her mom always had.

As the thoughts jostled around in her mind, Sky had one clear vision of the white stallion calling to her. If she could once again lay her hands on his strong neck, look into his defiant eyes, and absorb every hint of offered strength, then the horse magic would make her strong and steady. She had to be worthy of this gift – she would bestride her own life as fearlessly as she had ridden the unicorn; she would face the danger to earn incredible joy. And she would be strong.

She had to be strong...

"Hey, Sky!" Jeremy called again. "Any problems?"

"No! I just have to do something first."

She had to clean out what was rotten. Distastefully, Sky flushed the squirming decay down the toilet. Then she wrapped the moldy bags in toilet paper to be tossed into the garbage can out by the fence. With the thumb drive tucked into her pocket, she hurried downstairs.

"Your aunt left a note for you." Jeremy gestured to the kitchen table where a sheet of paper held a scrawled message.

Gone to the horse-breeding meeting. Back for dinner.

"Not an adult to be found," Jeremy muttered.

"We don't need them." Sky handed the thumb drive to Jeremy. "Maybe we should send this to the police after all."

"Yeah," he agreed slowly. "But I was thinking about how you said nobody ever believes you. We'd better make a copy in case someone officially stupid throws this away." He pushed the drive into his jeans pocket. "We need Athena. She's a pain but she's got a lot more computer expertise than me. Besides, the files might be encrypted. You know, like they always talk about on TV shows."

Sky shrugged. "I guess. I have some things to do anyway and I don't think even the Nightmare could get past Moose."

The dog sat back, panting happily, drool dripping from his lips. Jeremy laughed and with a wave left the house.

Sky watched until he had gone down the road toward Athena's house before she shot out the back door and ran for the pasture where the white stallion waited.

Would he be magic? Or just magnificent?

At the fence, she stopped and drank in the beauty of the land and the stallion. The horse stood brilliant white against the emerald green grass; a whicker of greeting floated to her. Sky scrambled over the fence, her hurry making her clumsy. Forgetting all caution, she ran to him. The horse backed up a few steps and tossed his head.

"Please help me," Sky pleaded. "He's come. The Nightmare is coming here..."

The sun shone over the stallion, but she couldn't tell if the light was simply glinting in her eyes, or if a sunlit horn gleamed from his forehead.

"Please," she repeated, arms outstretched.

The horse's head bobbed down. The breeze lifted his mane and tail in a swirl of beauty and magic as he stepped toward her.

With something like a sob, Sky put her arms around his neck, burying her face in his sweet horsey scent, feeling the velvet of his coat against her face.

"I need help," she whispered. "All the strength and magic you can give me. I have to find a way to beat the Nightmare or he'll destroy my family. I think he'll even destroy you too, somehow. He's like a maggot that feeds on rot and fouls everything. No beauty. No magic except maybe the worst kind. And I am so afraid."

It seemed as though a voice filled her mind. *You have fought hard, Dear Heart, and now I will give you my strength, too.*

As she breathed in the sweet horse scents, Sky felt herself lifting high into the clouds, once again galloping through mists, over waterfalls, and across plains. Sharing the magic of the unicorn's existence...

And then she was back in the pasture. The white stallion nuzzled her one more time and then walked slowly away to crop the new grass by the fence.

"All right, then." Sky whispered. She didn't know if she really felt any different. Not bigger or stronger – or if she only imagined it because she hungered so much for strength.

But she had to face the Nightmare.

Shakily, as she climbed back over the fence, she tried to make a plan. Any kind of plan. Hopeless. Sky faltered and stopped, fear paralyzing her legs. But then she heard the bugling neigh of the stallion and Moose pushed his head under her limp hand. And Jeremy and Athena were trying to decode the Nightmares files.

Maybe this time she wouldn't have to face the Nightmare alone.

When Sky returned to the farmhouse, Judy was watching the news with a steaming mug of tea beside her. At least the news was flickering on the TV screen, but her great-aunt's fingers drummed the side of the chair, and her frown seemed to send cold waves through the room.

Sky looked at her under lowered lashes and wondered how much, if anything, she should tell her about the Nightmare. How much could she risk?

"So, your mom called and left a message that she's decided to come back," Judy said sharply.

"What! No!" Sky cried out. "She can't! He's here. It's not safe."

"What's not safe?" Judy demanded. "I'm having just a little trouble wrapping my mind around her behavior. This is completely..."

"Stop it!" Sky shouted. "You don't understand. You can't understand!"

Judy stared at her, face stiffening even more. "Oh really? Then maybe you would be good enough to explain. This isn't a hotel with a revolving door," she began again. "Not that Lindey ever thought twice about anyone!"

"Will you shut up!" Sky hissed. "You don't get it. It's the Nightmare! He's found me. If mom comes back, he might...he might kill her. Kill us both."

"Oh really? You can stop exaggerating, Sky. I don't need any teen drama," Judy snapped. "What or who is the Nightmare?"

"This isn't drama," Sky took a long shuddering breath. "You saw the bruises on mom's face. You heard the medics say I had experienced 'past trauma!' Where do you think that came from? Why do you think mom left me and then just drove away?"

"I have no idea," Judy retorted. "If this is just some stunt..."

Sky curled her hands into fists. "Why do you hang on to the mistakes mom made when she was a teenager? She isn't a teenager now and she's running for her life."

"That sounds awfully far-fetched, Sky." Judy's voice had dropped, but her scowl had edged more toward bewilderment.

Sky didn't care. She'd had it with pretending to be some good little girl. "And she didn't even dare tell you she has a psycho after us because you are so sure she's only thinking about herself. You don't know..."

Sky's head pounded with the passion that was finally exploding in her. The rage. The gasping fear. The Nightmare had found her.

The Nightmare had found her.

Chapter 18

Sky dropped into an armchair and put her head in her hands. The only sounds in the room were the newscaster's chirpy account of a disaster and her own harsh breathing. A moment later, the voice cut off mid-sentence as Judy switched off the TV.

"What's going on, Sky?" her great-aunt demanded. "The truth, please."

Sky didn't move for long seconds, and then finally lifted her head. "Mom and me are running from her old boyfriend. He is...abusive. Very, very abusive. And possessive. We've tried to get away before but he always found us." Her voice began to shake, but she wrapped her arms around herself and kept going. "Mom thought I might be safe with you...that the horse magic might protect me." Sky laughed bitterly. "She's trying to get far enough away that he won't find her...us. Or if he found her, he wouldn't find me. She's been trying to save us..."

"That's nonsense," Judy said, but her voice lacked certainty. "Why didn't she go to the police?"

"Because they never believe us," Sky said her voice low. "He looks like an upstanding citizen and after...after the hurting, he doesn't let us out of the house until there's nothing to show. And everyone...likes him. Thinks he's amazing...and mom just sounds crazy." Sky glared. "Even you, her aunt, thought she was just being a drama queen."

Judy's cheeks reddened. "I'm sorry, Sky. I'm so sorry." She rubbed her hand across her forehead. "But you're here. And you're safe. When your mom comes back, I'll keep her safe too. I promise." She forced a laugh. "The unicorn magic has worn pretty thin these days, but I swear we'll make our own magic if we have to."

Moose woofed. "I know, Moose, you've got our backs," Judy tried for a lighter note. "Have you seen this...this Nightmare?" she asked. "Did you spot him hanging around?"

Sky shook her head. "But...I know he's found me."

"If you haven't seen him," Judy said, standing up. "It might just be anxiety talking. And I guarantee he won't be showing up here without Moose taking a bite out of him." She paused. "I think it's smart for you to keep Moose with you when you go out. In the meantime, give me the information about this Nightmare and I'll alert the police about it."

Sky gestured at the futility. "There is nothing to give," she said. "He looks ordinary. Dark hair, medium height. He uses aliases all the time so I don't even know his real name."

Judy's brows rose. "Not much to go on."

Sky's temper flared. "If it was easy, we would have already fixed it."

Judy nodded, the frown settling again on her expression. "Okay. I'll think on it. I'll at least notify the police of something."

Sky watched her move into the kitchen. Judy didn't, *couldn't*, understand the malignance that radiated from the Nightmare.

And even her aunt admitted the unicorn magic had worn thin. Sky stared down at her hands, remembering the velvet feel of the horse's coat, the grass-scented warmth of his breath. Maybe the stallion...the unicorn... would keep building magic in her. With a tremor of fear, she realized that magic or not, she didn't have enough of anything to win against the Nightmare.

And the unicorn? That horse had been penned and starved himself. How strong could his magic really be?

Dinner was quiet. Plates of microwave-heated, packaged meatballs and bottled spaghetti poured liberally over pasta. For once Sky didn't care how much was her rightful share. Having erupted in anger, she somehow had room for the food her body craved. Judy paid no attention, seeming lost in her own thoughts.

"Tomorrow," Judy said, as they cleared up the meal, "I have another meeting of this so-called breeding consortium. Then I'll see what the police can do. Surely they can do something – that's what I pay my ridiculous taxes for anyway. But I don't want you to go anywhere without Moose and I really would prefer you just stay home."

Sky nodded as if agreeing, but even though she fully intended to take Moose with her, she had to find out if Jeremy and Athena had done anything with the thumb drive. She wondered if she should have told her aunt about it. But Aunt Judy already thought her mother was stupid and she'd think Sky had taken a stupid chance too.

And maybe she wouldn't be wrong, Sky thought bitterly. For the time being she'd keep the existence of the thumb drive to herself.

Later, in her room, Sky knelt at the window, gazing out at the stars, wondering where her mom was, wishing she had some way to contact her and warn her to stay away. Across the road and fields, she saw a light flare at the top floor of Jeremy's house. Maybe it was her cousin up there. Maybe he was coming up with a plan that would protect her.

"Better be something amazing." Sky ran her hand over Moose's soft head and rubbed his ears. "But maybe he's just crashing. Have you got any great ideas, Moose?"

The dog woofed softly. "Yeah, I know. It's up to me." Sky laid her cheek against his head. "Maybe I just need to tap into the unicorn magic again. If there's any magic left to tap into."

Sky listened impatiently as her aunt's regular bedtime ritual played out. And then silence. Her own breathing quickened. She needed to go back to the horse, coax out all the magic within. There had to be more magic – she needed so much more.

But she could feel the Nightmare's evil oozing through the night. Reaching for her...

"Get a grip, Sky," she ordered herself. "Right now, he's probably ordering room service in some five star hotel somewhere. There's no reason at all, he'd be out there..."

She waited in the dark a little longer. How was she going to fill herself with magic? The story said her great-great grandmother earned it when she had faced down the ranchers and walked straight into the herd of panicking wild horses. Sky wondered if her ancestor's legs had shaken in fear.

"They must have. She must have been terrified," Sky whispered to Moose. "But she tried to save them anyway."

Briefly Sky wondered if her great-great grandmother had ever been the victim of cruelty as she had. Had she ever been a helpless victim before she summoned such courage?

"Doesn't matter, though, does it Moose?" Sky said softly. "I have to try, anyway." Ignoring her too-fast breathing and her shaking hands, Sky pulled on her jacket and shoes, and silently crept down the stairs. Moose padded behind her.

Outside, the air crisped and the moon shone magically silver across the garden. Dark shadows stretched into eerie proportions. Sky ghosted across the landscape, hiding her presence.

Her family had lived here for generations. Were her long-dead forebears watching her in the night? Were they ranged beside her, calling up their love and courage for the fight against the Nightmare's evil? Or was she completely alone in this?

Goosebumps rose on her skin as Sky jogged through the damp undergrowth toward the pasture, her breath quickening. She felt the pull of the magic, the thrill of excitement as she reached the pasture. It would be okay. The horse would make everything okay.

But the field was empty.

A low moan escaped her. Sky slid down to the ground, wrapping her arms protectively around herself. Moose huffed and plumped down beside her.

"Where?" she muttered thickly. Luridly, she pictured the Nightmare throwing a noose around the unicorn's head, cutting off the glimmering horn, dragging away the magical creature…

"Think!" she commanded herself. Why would the Nightmare want the stallion? No way Neil would let a stranger take the horse.

Desperate, Sky forced herself to her feet. She moved silently, circling around the fenced fields, sending soft reassurance to the horses still moving around the other pastures. At the center of the property stood Neil's barns and training arena. Like a phantom, Sky passed through the night, moving closer and closer to the structures.

Muffled voices and periodic thumps echoed from inside the nearest building. The barn door stood open, dim light showing the interior.

"Stay," she hissed to Moose and edged into the shadows by the door.

Neil and one of his men stood in front of a box stall where intermittent crashes shook the boards and rattled the shovels, brooms, and pitchforks hung on nearby walls.

"You sure about this one, boss?" the hired hand asked. He seemed to be nursing his arm.

"I couldn't leave him in the field forever," Neil answered. "And this horse is the best stud I'll ever have. If this consortium is a go, he'll make me a lot of money."

"If he don't kill someone first," the hand said bitterly.

Neil shrugged. "Do you want me to drive you over to the emergency room? Get that arm looked at?"

"Naw. I'll wrap it up good and if it looks bad in the morning, I'll give my doctor a call."

Neil nodded. "I'll cover the bill. Just let me know."

Together the two men walked toward the door. Behind them, the boards of the stall thumped and juddered where the stallion kicked his rage. Outside the door, Sky slid further back into the shadows, keeping her head down and hoping the men would not see or sense her presence. But they were too busy talking about their plans for the breeding consortium while they closed up the barn. Sky watched them walk toward Neil's house and the nearby trailers that housed his men. When they had disappeared, she carefully unlatched the door again and slid into the barn. The unmistakable scent of hay and horse filled her nostrils and she stood a moment in the velvet dark to orient herself.

And then...a glimmer of light shone from a stall. Sky pressed back a small sob of relief and ran to the horse. In the intense dark, the horn shone from the beautiful creature's forehead. He whickered a greeting as Sky unlatched the stall door and rushed to put her arms around his gleaming white neck.

"I thought I'd lost you," she whispered. "And I know the Nightmare is coming. I have to beat him somehow. I need your help. If there's any magic left at all, now is the time to share."

The unicorn nuzzled her hair. Once again, she felt the flow of warm strength and surety. Once again, she breathed in the goodness that rose like a beacon, dispelling fear.

Sky sighed, wished she could just break the horse out of the barn and ride away to... anywhere. To someplace magical and safe and beautiful.

"This is your place, Dear Heart," whispered in her mind. *"You have come home at last to those who love you. This is your true strength."*

"No! That's not good enough. You don't know how bad he is – please, please help me!" Sky begged, looking up into the liquid eyes.

The shimmering light of the horn faded and disappeared. The horse turned away and began to lip at the trough full of hay. Sky stood alone in the dark, bereft.

"Okay then," she said bitterly. "If that's all you've got. Okay…"

She left the stall, slamming the gate behind her, stumbling a little in the inky shadows. "So take your magic and shove it!"

She would not cry. She would not give in. She hadn't given in to the evil of the Nightmare, and she would not give in to the useless hope of rescue.

"I'll save myself," she shot back at the stallion. "And my mother, too. I'll do it myself."

The horse whinnied and went back to chomping hay.

Sky left the barn and angrily shoved the door shut, latching it with a clang. Who cared if Neil or anyone else heard her? Who cared about anyone or anything?

She had sprinted a hundred yards along the path behind the fields before she realized Moose was not at her side.

"Damn dog," she muttered softly. "You'd better not be chasing rabbits." She turned back toward the barn, moving cautiously in the dark. A moment later, she suddenly felt Moose's warmth pressing tightly against her legs. The dog blocked her movement and a menacing rumble rose from his throat.

"Moose?" Sky whispered. "What?"

The low growl continued. Sky looked around, confused. A tingle of fear shot up her spine.

And then she saw it. On the farthest side of the fields, the tip of a cigar glowed in the shadows.

A mewl of animal fear choked in Sky's throat. *He was here*. The Nightmare really was here....

Sky forced her shaking legs to carry her back into the shadows, to run gasping toward the farmhouse and the hope of safety.

The Nightmare had found her.

How long before his game of cat and mouse was over and she was back in his power? How long before he caught her?

Chapter 19

Hands shaking so hard she could barely turn the handle, Sky slipped into the dark kitchen with Moose still rumbling threats in his throat. She pushed the door shut and slammed the locks down. For a moment she leaned against the wall, panting like a hunted animal, and then tore around the rest of the house ensuring that every possible door and window was closed and locked. That done, she stumbled up to her bedroom and without any light except that of the moon shining in her window, undressed and slipped shuddering into bed.

Should she wake Judy and demand... *what?* That her aunt call the police because, while trespassing again, Sky had seen a cigar tip glowing in the night?

The doors were locked. The windows were locked. Moose lay beside her. For now, for this moment, she was safe.

And then what? Ideas, fears, and memories swirled feverishly in her mind. What had happened...what might happen...what he would do to her...tangled into a waking nightmare. But then somehow, exhaustion won and Sky slipped into dreams.

With limbs almost too weak to stand, she tries to hoist herself onto the back of the unicorn. She has to climb on. Has to gallop away from evil...but she keeps slipping and falling.

"Don't give up, Dear One," the unicorn whispers to her. "You have all the strength of your heart."

Weeping, Sky tries again and miraculously the creature turns its head, so that the horn becomes a step that boosts her onto his shimmering back. She winds her fingers into his mane as he leaps upward into the mist. Once again she rides the unicorn through the moonlit sky. Far below, she sees her mother's old car driving through a mountain pass.

"Go back!" Sky tries to call, but her voice is lost in the wind.

Fields, mountains, woods, and waterfalls pass beneath her and the unicorn. Sky hears the cry of a hunting owl, sees coyotes pass swiftly through the shadows, spies herds of elk settling into slumber. The magic of the land rises up and echoes within her. It seems as if she can hear the language of the creatures and of nature itself, can feel herself woven into the fabric of the earth, both the seen and unseen. Her heart beats in the same rhythms. With the unicorn's powerful hooves carrying her across the world, her fear becomes small and slips away. Love and courage grow upwards in their place until the mists float her back to her bed.

When Sky awoke, the sun streamed into the room, bathing her face. For a moment she basked in the feeling of well-being, of surging hope.

But her head ached and she heard the ordinary sounds of Judy moving around in the kitchen. The dream faded before reality, and as the enchantment ebbed, the terror grew. The Nightmare's inevitability crashed back over her.

In cold daylight, there was no magic. There was no help but what she built around herself. Sky paused. What she had built, and now what her friends and aunt helped prop up.

Flimsy. Like a house of sticks.

"Running away was a house of straw," she murmured to Moose. "So I've upgraded to sticks...how can I get some bricks?"

The aroma of coffee and toasting bread rose up the stairs, inviting, but Sky stayed where she was, too afraid to face the day.

Moose thrust his head under her hand, clearly urging her to go explore the smells below. Sky turned away, pulling up the blankets. Moose made a sound like a mournful sigh and settled sadly, his great head resting on the side of the bed.

"You don't have to guard me until you starve," Sky hissed at him.

Moose sighed again and his nose bunted at the bundle of blankets.

In spite of it all, a smile tugged at Sky's mouth. Reluctantly, she pushed back the covers and swung her legs out of bed. "My safety is entirely in your paws," Sky told him. "Got any bricks handy?"

Once showered and dressed, Sky joined Judy at the table. Her aunt was impatiently shuffling papers and tapping a pencil against her teeth. Sky poured herself some coffee and watched disinterestedly. As soon as she could get away, she had to see Athena and Jeremy – find out if Athena could decode the flash drive and its files.

"Everything adds up," Judy muttered. "But this doesn't seem..." She frowned and shuffled the documents again.

"Are you going to the consortium meeting again?" Sky asked.

"Uh huh." Judy sighed and slipped the papers into a folder. "Neil has set it up over in his indoor arena. This guy, Daryl Hammett, has ordered in some fancy lunch and is going to go over the plans and numbers again. He's got about twelve folks interested – at ten thousand apiece. Crazy." Judy sat back. "I don't know why I'm getting suckered into this, except I miss horses. But I was so angry and half-crippled after my fall that I sold every one of my animals. All to great places where they'd be treated well, but damn, I miss them. I was too hasty."

"Seems to run in the family," Sky replied.

Judy gave a half laugh. "You're not wrong there. Neil offered to look out for my horses until I was on my feet, but I turned him down. I have too much useless pride. My only excuse is he's an infuriating man and my brains must've been rattled by the fall."

Sky laughed. Judy picked up the papers and shoved them into a bag. "Keep Moose with you," she advised. "Make sure you lock up if you go out, and if you need me, I'm in the second barn."

"I'll be careful." Sky hesitated. "Did mom say when she'd be back here?"

Judy shook her head. "No, and she called from a pubic phone at a rest stop somewhere so there's no way to get hold of her. I checked." She gripped her great-niece's shoulder. "Don't worry. She'll be safe here. We'll keep her safe."

Sky nodded and tried to school her face into bland passivity. There had been no safety for a long time, and Judy's assurances might be well meant, but her aunt had no conception of the extent of the Nightmare's malevolence.

Once Judy's car started and drove out the driveway, Sky grabbed a slice of toast, and eating while she walked, hurried toward Athena's house with Moose at her heels.

Her friend's home was the first in a small enclave built on subdivided farmland. Sky jogged up to the door and rapped sharply.

A woman with Athena's same curly dark hair opened the door. "Hi there!" she almost chirped. "It's good to see you looking so well, Sky. You certainly had us all worried after your accident! Are you all better now?"

Sky stifled her irritation and assumed the friendly, positive expression people liked. "I'm fine. Thank you. Is Athena here?"

"Oh yes," Mrs. Faviola exclaimed. "She and that nice boy, Jeremy, are upstairs." She gestured toward an uncarpeted wooden stairway. "Athena, precious!" she called. "Your friend is here!"

Thumps on the upper floor heralded Athena's arrival. "Thanks, Mom. Come on up, Sky!"

"Stay!" Sky ordered Moose. "I'll be back soon."

When Sky reached her friend, Athena forced a smile as fake as her own had been. "My mom travels a lot," she said. "She hasn't noticed I'm old enough to drive. Just ignore her and she'll go away again in a week or two."

Sky stifled a laugh and followed Athena into an office with three desks, dominated by a scanner and three huge computer monitors. Jeremy grunted a greeting and leaned forward again to stare at files that were spread across the screens.

"I'm not sure what I'm looking at," he told Athena. "A lot of spreadsheets. A lot of names and numbers that don't make any sense."

Athena nodded glumly. "I decoded the encryption – it was actually very basic – anyone can get the software. The key was the password but Sky gave me enough info to guess. The guy is a mystery nut and really not a nice man, ergo, Moriarty."

"Wow," Jeremy jibed. "I didn't know you were that smart, Athena."

"That's because all you pay attention to is your dumb horses." Athena gestured to the array of digital files. "But I don't know what all of this means."

Sky stared silently at the names on the files. Her eyes scanned dates and notes. "I know what this is," she said. "These are the scams he's run. He bragged about them to mom when he'd been drinking. I don't know how they worked or how he got people to hand over their money, but he did it. Over and over again." She drew a harsh breath. "He will kill me to get this back."

Silence but for the rasping sound of Sky's breathing. She knew she was trembling again but forced herself to stay upright, gripping the back of the chair.

"There's a sucker born every minute," Athena muttered. "And I think your Nightmare found most of them."

Jeremy rubbed his big hand over his face. "We need to give this to the police," he said. "If the information is out there, he's got no reason to come after you, Sky. Can you send the files to the authorities, Athena? Without the encryption?"

"Of course," she replied. "And the FBI. I think it needs to go to the FBI."

"Right." Jeremy got to his feet. "You get on that."

"Don't think I won't," Athena retorted and slid into one of the chairs.

"What should we do now?" Sky asked. Positive. Stay positive. Ignore the sense of quicksand pulling her into nothingness. She watched as Athena hummed to herself and started typing. "The police never listened to us before, so why should they now?" Sky said. "At least not before he disappears again. Then he'll just get a new identity anyway..." She sat down hard in a chair, wondering what he would do to her. "I think...it's pretty much hopeless."

Athena swiveled and touched her arm. "Not hopeless," she insisted. "Just hard. I'll do what I can to make all these files pop out at the authorities. Maybe the media." She turned back to the screen. "And I'm good enough to make it happen."

Sky rolled her eyes but not knowing what else to do stood to leave. Jeremy frowned. "I think first thing is we start telling everyone. Your aunt, my dad, for starters. We'll have to go interrupt that meeting to do it, but that's life. Knowledge is power and the more people who share the knowledge, the less power one person has." He gripped Sky's arm. "We'll keep you safe. Promise."

"And get that scum-sucking creep," Athena added.

They didn't know, Sky thought dully. How could they know what the Nightmare was? She swallowed. "I didn't tell you, but I'm pretty sure I saw the Nightmare last night. I don't know if he saw me, but if he's here..."

Athena's hands stilled on the keyboard. "I'm sorry, Sky. I didn't..."

Sky shrugged and forced a smile. "It's not a big deal. How could you even imagine? And... and I know him. He wouldn't quit until he found me."

"Let's go," Jeremy urged. "We'll stick together. Me and Moose will make pretty good bodyguards."

They left Athena working at the computer, called to Moose when they left the house, and headed back toward McClelland's barn.

"I'm not sure what to tell people," Sky said nervously.

"The truth is a start," Jeremy replied. He pointed at the arena where a gaudy sign announcing the meeting had been strung across the open door. "My guess is they're in there," he said wryly.

Sky's steps faltered. "Wait," she said. "I want...I need to see my horse."

"Sky!" Jeremy expostulated, but it was too late. Sky took off toward the barn, needing desperately to find her unicorn, to draw strength from his warmth and beauty...his magic. In all this fear and dreary pain, she needed magic. It didn't matter any more that she had doubts about it. It mattered that she was willing to believe in something good. She had to believe in goodness. She had to.

She ran into the barn, skidding to a stop before the box stall where her horse had been housed last night. The wooden door was splintered and the stall itself showed cracks.

Empty.

Her breathing rasped in her throat again. The horse was gone. Had the Nightmare somehow caught him? Harmed him?

Think, Sky screamed at herself. The goodness had to be stronger than evil. It had to be. The stall was ruined. Maybe the stallion was back in the pasture?

She ran out of the barn and ladder climbed one of the fences to gain a vantage point. No gleam of white shone against the emerald grass and jade trees anywhere. There was no sign of the stallion.

"Where are you?" Sky cried into the air.

"Sky!" Jeremy's voice boomed out. Sky shook her head. She had to find the horse... She closed her eyes, willing her mind and heart to reach out to the creature.

She felt his anger and defiance. Here. He was near her, after all.

"Sky!" Jeremy reached her and grabbed her arm. "Stay with the plan," he urged.

"There isn't a plan unless I can save the stallion," Sky yelled. "I know the Nightmare is here. I can't let him hurt my horse."

"No sense. You are making no sense," Jeremy argued.

Sky shook her head. She felt as though all the pieces had started clicking together in her mind, like a puzzle that spun around and around on tumblers and then one by one locked into place to reveal the answer. The Nightmare spewed evil into the world. She had been only one of his victims. The unicorn glowed with goodness. She would take the path the unicorn laid out. Hope surged in her again.

She had to find him.

"I know it sounds crazy," she told Jeremy, her voice rapid and strong now. "But it's like the horse and me are joined. If I don't save him, I won't save myself either."

"Loony tunes," Jeremy muttered. "But can we take a moment to tell your aunt and my dad about those files?"

Sky looked around the pasture. No horse... but he was near. "Yes," she said. "And then we find out what happened to the stallion."

"Good enough," Jeremy agreed.

They ran towards the arena. Jeremy's dad's voice, magnified by a sound system floated out on the air.

"I, for one, am convinced that this consortium is our one chance, a great chance, to get into the big time..." he was saying.

Jeremy grimaced, but led the way into the barn. A resounding crash cut off the speech.

"We found your horse." Jeremy pointed to the end of the arena where a podium had been set up...and the stallion put on display.

Neil struggled to hold onto the horse's bridle as the animal plunged and sidled. Sawdust formed a golden halo as the enraged stallion bucked and kicked, slashing at the men and the podium. Jeremy's dad dove away as the rear hooves connected to the wood and the sound system's amplifiers flew into the air.

Neil yelled commands and struggled to pull the horse down, but the creature yanked himself free and reared, pawing the air. Galloping forward, the stallion slashed at the men. Neil and Roger Stolz vaulted over the boards and just made it to safety. Turning back to the podium, the horse pounded the wood to tinder, and then bugled his fury.

Maddened, he galloped wildly around the ring, slowing only to kick at the boards.

"No!" Sky screamed. He would hurt himself! Break his legs in this crazed defiance.

She tore past Jeremy and threw herself over the boards into the arena. Dimly she heard her aunt and others shouting for her to get to safety. But her eyes and heart were entirely on the stallion.

"I'm here," she said clearly. "I'm here and I'll keep you safe...I promise."

The stallion slowed to a trot, tossing his head, neighing in rage. Sky stepped toward him, hands outstretched. "I've made you a promise," she said. "And I'll keep it. I'll keep my word."

It was as though she could see two horses, the magnificent stallion and the unicorn, blended into one creature. Horse magic that had called her. This was her heritage after all.

"It's okay," Sky said. The trembling horse slowed, shoulders quivering, and walked toward her. She raised her hands to stroke his nose and cheeks, to caress the velvet neck.

"Let me bring you somewhere safe," Sky whispered. The horse whickered and bunted her with his elegant head.

She clasped the bridle and turned around leading the stallion toward the gate.

The people watched silently, frozen, until one man began clapping – a slow, rhythmic echo in the arena.

"Impressive," he called. His perfectly toned voice filled the air.

"*Stupid!*" Sky heard Aunt Judy sharply correct him.

Sky stopped moving, stopped breathing. The horse gently pushed his nose against her back, urging her forward. But like every watcher, except one, she froze.

"Good work, Sky!" Neil McClelland leaned forward on the boards and gestured to the man beside him. "You need to meet Daryl Hammett, the force behind our new consortium. I'd bet he could find a spot for someone with your horse magic!"

"Yes, I can definitely find a spot for her," the man said, smooth smile lightening his handsome face. He pushed open the gate and strolled down toward the horse and girl.

The world spun; Sky's knees buckled. The Nightmare watched with his ice chip eyes as she fainted silently into the sawdust.

226   Susan Brown

Chapter 20

Sky's eyes fluttered open. Her heart felt like cold lead, thudding painfully against her ribs. Above her she saw the gleaming chest of the stallion, his legs spread so that his hooves rested in the sawdust on each side of her.

"Will you get out of my way!" she heard Judy exclaim. Her aunt shoved Neil aside, and ignoring the horse standing sentinel, dropped to her knees beside her great-niece. "I hate drama," she muttered. "Sky, what's wrong?"

Sky fought back the hysterical sobs trying to wrack her frame. "Him," she managed. "Nightmare."

"What? Who?" Judy looked around her at the people clustering closer.

Jeremy laid one big hand on the horse's chest and leaned down towards his cousin. "Him?" he demanded. "It's that guy?"

Despite the trembling that shook her, Sky answered loudly. "Yes...don't let..."

The stallion suddenly raised his head and neighed a challenge, ears back, teeth gleaming. Silence fell. The stallion bugled again. A shaft of light shot across the sawdust, as the outer door opened and then swung closed again.

Fists clenched, Jeremy ran across the floor but the Nightmare had slipped away. "Dad!" he shouted, "that guy's a con man! He's after Sky!"

His father stood bewildered. "Jeremy, but…"

"Knew it was too damn good to be true," Judy hissed. "Are you hurt, Sky? Can you get up?" Awkwardly, she stood herself and gave Sky a hand to get to her feet, supporting herself unconsciously with her other hand on the gleaming white chest. The horse nickered and blew hot breath across her.

"I'm okay…really…" Sky stood up, leaning against the horse's shoulder, her hand tightly holding onto her aunt's.

She could see Jeremy gesturing and talking earnestly to Neil and his dad. Their wide eyes swung toward her, and their expressions shifted from incredulity to anger. Neil and Jeremy broke away and strode over to her.

"Is this true?" he demanded of Sky.

"Oh, be quiet, Neil," Judy snapped. "You have eyes and my girl needs to get home – despite you and your precious schemes."

Sky took a couple of steps with her aunt and then turned. "My horse," she insisted. "What are you going to do with him?"

Neil eyed the now calm animal skeptically. "I'll get him in a stall somehow and look after him fine, Sky. Don't worry." He flinched a bit when the horse's ears twitched.

"He's laughing at you," Jeremy said. He took the stallion's bridle and looked at the great animal. "Come on, then. I'm only half Whitmore, but I got enough magic in me to help you out," he told the horse. Confidently, he turned toward the gate, and with a flick of his tail, the horse trotted after him.

"Got his mother's way with horses," Roger Stolz said with clear pride.

Judy held tight to Sky as they walked to her car. The shuddering that had overtaken her was easing and Sky forced herself to walk with her back straight. Not a victim. She would never be a victim again – no matter how much fear she carried.

Back at the house, Judy fussed around, muttering about idiotic men and making mugs of sweet tea while Sky sat at the table, head in hands, forcing herself to think.

"It's not over," Sky interrupted. "Just because I outed him, it isn't over. He's vindictive, and he'll do something, anything, to not be beaten."

Judy's hand stilled in the act of piling cookies onto a plate. "Why? Is he truly that malicious?"

Sky touched the nearly healed burns on her upper arm. "Yes," she said. "At first, when he hurt mom or me, he would act sorry afterwards. Big presents. Once he even cried when mom said she wanted to leave. But it was all an act. When she realized we couldn't leave, that he always found us, he stopped acting sorry. He likes power, likes to hurt. He'll come back at us somehow. Especially me."

Judy plunked the cookies down and took a long breath. "Why especially you?"

"I took a thumb drive that has file copies of the scams he's run. I thought…I hoped it might keep him away or send him to jail or something." Sky turned the hot mug between her palms. "It was dumb. Really dumb."

"Where are these files now?" Judy asked.

"I gave them to Athena. She's forwarding them to the police."

Judy picked up a cookie and dunked it in her tea, watching absently as it crumbled and drifted to the bottom of the cup. "Then maybe he'll just disappear."

Sky shook her head. "He'll get back at me. He'll…"

A knock sounded sharply on the door. Sky suppressed a cry and Judy hesitated for an instant, but when Moose's loud bark simply announced a friend, she hurried to open it.

"*Lindey!*" Sky heard her exclaim. "Your timing is terrible."

Sky saw her mom hesitate by the door. The bruises on her cheek and jaw had faded but her face was pale and drawn.

"I'm sorry, Aunt Judy," she murmured. "I'm sorry. But I just can't run any more. Is Sky okay?"

"Yes," Judy snapped, pushing the door shut and in a smooth motion, pulling Lindey into a hug. "Why didn't you tell me, you silly girl?"

"Because I'm not a girl," Lindey said. "And I made my bed..."

"Yes," Judy said, "but that doesn't mean you have to practically die in it. Family, Lindey. No matter what, we're family."

Sky watched as her mom clung wordlessly to her aunt. She felt distanced, almost without emotion, because she knew that the Nightmare would be planning revenge. He didn't forget, he certainly never forgave, and above all, he would not allow himself to be beaten. How soon? How soon would it begin? And what would happen to her magical horse? The Nightmare would target whatever would hurt her the most.

The rest of the afternoon passed in futile scurries of activity. Judy called the police, threw the phone down and then called Neil.

She threw the phone down again. Both Athena and Jeremy arrived after lunch, Athena full of plans and Jeremy silent and worried.

"I sent files to *everyone!*" Athena declared. "With attachments and pop-ups and high priority notices. Police. State Patrol. FBI. Everyone!"

"Anyone answer?" Jeremy growled.

"They will," Athena responded. "But I suppose even they have to have time to process things."

"My dad has been down to the police station. He and Neil filed a complaint and turned over all their documents," Jeremy offered.

"It won't prove anything," Sky said dully. "The references will be fake. The bank accounts are dummies. It'll be a maze of dead ends."

Her mother nodded and dropped her eyes. "He always covers his bases," she agreed. "Always has a back-up plan...or six. It's why he made so much money...why he's been so hard to stop."

"He's a man," Judy interrupted impatiently. "Everyone..." she looked at her niece, "everyone makes a mistake sometimes. What matters is what that person does next."

"And we don't know what he'll do next," Jeremy said glumly. "Maybe nothing...at least for awhile."

They finally left. Sky, her mom, and great-aunt watched a mesmerizingly silly comedy on TV and then with a lot of hugs and rather desperately silly jokes, all three went to bed. Sky didn't undress, but rather sat on the edge of her bed, stroking Moose's large head, staring out into the night.

She could feel him out there. Feel his evil spreading like a disease across the beautiful land. And she could feel the light that came from the unicorn as it silently resisted that evil. She felt as though two blankets lapped over her, one of evil, one of good. She was the meeting point.

"What am I doing sitting here?" she murmured to Moose.

The night was so dark and she was so tired. How long had she been trying to fight the Nightmare? And losing. Maybe he would just go away and forget about them. Cut his losses this one time and run.

Sky laughed, a bitter, hopeless sound even to herself.

Out there, the evil was oozing toward her unicorn. She knew it. And she wanted so much to crawl into bed and pull the blankets over her head. To stay safe in the farmhouse with Moose and her great-aunt to guard her.

"Damn," she muttered and forced herself to her feet. She rooted in her closet for a warm jacket and with a sigh, slipped down the stairs, and out into the night. As if sensing the danger, Moose padded silently behind her, never more than a few feet away.

The unicorn waited. She wouldn't let him wait alone.

Chapter 21

The shadows were long and the air chill as Sky jogged toward the stable that housed the stallion. As she went, she wondered if the white horse was truly a unicorn. Or had he somehow captured the unicorn's elemental magic?

"Doesn't matter much, does it?" she murmured to Moose.

He barked once in response, and loped beside her.

As Sky had expected, the pasture was empty. She ran along the fences that bounded Neil's fields, heading toward the barn. Distantly, a wildly beeping cacophony of alarms split the night.

And then she stopped. Frozen. Tongues of flame were licking at the edges of the barn doors. Oily black smoke had begun to rise from the vents in the roof. The night air felt acrid in her lungs.

Sky shouted for help. Moose howled as panicked neighs and rising shrieks of terrified horses shattered the still night.

"Fire!" Sky screamed. *"Fire!"* She ran full tilt towards the barn, yelling as she went. Until a hand shot out of the night and grabbed her

"Not so fast, Sky," an icy voice whispered. "We have some business to take care of."

The steel hand gripped her shoulder. As Sky stared into the Nightmare's face, he snapped open his lighter. The tiny flame danced closer and closer to her cheek. Paralysis seized Sky's limbs...she couldn't breathe...terrible animal panting hissed from her lips.

As she felt herself sinking down, the bugling cry of the white horse shattered the night. The vise of fear that held Sky broke open.

"No!' she yelled. Fighting back with every ounce of her strength, flailing and digging at the evil face looming over her, Sky yanked backwards. His hands clawed into her skin. She kept fighting even as the pain spiked ever higher. And then his hold suddenly weakened. The Nightmare howled and let go.

Breathing hard, barely able to stand, Sky staggered backward. In the lurid light of the fire she saw him hobble, arms punching ineffectively at Moose. The dog's snarls crescendoed and his fangs tore into the man's leg.

For an instant, Sky hoped her dog would kill him. Maim him...

"Moose! Leave it!" Sky shouted. "Leave him...we have to get the horses. The fire's gaining in the barn!"

With another snarl, Moose let the Nightmare go. Leaving him writhing in the grass, Sky and the dog ran toward the barn. Her warning and the alarms had been heard. Lights flicked on in Neil's house and the hands' trailers. Shouts echoed as doors slammed open and men ran out, hastily pulling on jackets.

For what seemed hours, the men pulled out hoses, sprayed fire extinguishers, shouted orders, tried to beat the flames down, but they couldn't get the conflagration under control. The fire had been started in too many places.

The flames licked around the barn's old wood and rose into the night.

Desperate, Sky ran to the big doors and swung them wide.

"Wait!" Neil shouted.

A wall of heat and smoke nearly knocked her over. Flames crackled in stacked bales of hay and the horses screamed and kicked in terror.

Sky threw open stall doors, burning her palms on the hot latches. The horses, mad with panic, reared and twisted but did not run for safety. Beside her Neil and his men were grabbing the animals, pulling their halters.

"It ain't gonna work, boss." One of the hands yelled. "This place is going to go!"

In the far distance, Sky heard the wail of sirens. Her horse. She had to save her horse.

She plunged into the smoke, calling out. There. At the back. The last stall where the flames burst upward.

Her unicorn. Her horse.

"I'm coming!" she shouted. Hands burning, Sky tore at the stall's gate until she had it open. The unicorn, horn shimmering, stood almost motionless, with only his flicking tail and shivering shoulders gleaming in the smoke and firelight.

"I'm here," Sky crooned. Without thought, she spider-crawled up the stall and vaulted onto his back. She dug her blistered fingers into his mane and held on as he reared.

"We can do this," she shouted. "We'll save them."

The unicorn bounded forward, neighing shrilly through the fire and smoke. The laboring men fell back as he rushed forward. The horse neighed again, a fierce call, and the panicked creatures in the stalls turned and streamed out after him.

Sky and the horse galloped forward, into the night, toward the waiting pastures. She saw Aunt Judy and her mom, night clothes streaming in the wind, throwing open the pasture gates to receive the desperate animals. Jeremy and his dad were pulling in the strays, running hands over limping animals. Athena and her parents were dashing around making a lot of noise. Her dad was on his phone.

As the fire department arrived and turned their hoses on the flaming barn, Sky and the unicorn jumped over the far fence, into the shadows. For just a moment, Sky felt the peace of the horse magic, the rightness of its nature wash over her. Wondering, she held up her hands. The blisters were fading and the pain easing.

And then the night cracked open.

He was there. The distant, dying flames highlighted the Nightmare's contorted face. He grabbed Sky's leg, pulling her viciously downward. The unicorn shrilled as the Nightmare drove a pitchfork at his chest.

"No!" Sky screamed and threw herself forward, all her weight and strength on the man's arm. Viciously he punched her, tried to maneuver the pitchfork to stab her. She fought back, wrestling and fighting to protect herself and the unicorn. She was down, the tines poised above her as malevolence shone in the Nightmare's face.

She rolled. Above her the gleaming white horse reared and his hooves crashed down on the man's shoulders, knocking him to the ground. His face twisted in pain and terror; then he lay frozen in the mud, too terrified to move. Moose bounded from the night and stood guard, growling deep in his chest. The stallion neighed in defiance once more, and then trotted slowly toward the trees.

Sky looked down at the man. Saw that he was only a man, a stupidly too-clever criminal. No longer her Nightmare. She had defeated him. With friends and courage, she had defeated him.

The unicorn's magic throbbed in her veins, hard-earned. A part of her forever.

"Hey!" Sky turned and shouted. "Neil! Aunt Judy! Get the police! We've got him."

Her great-aunt and Neil left the settling horses and ran towards them.

"Well, look what we've got here," Neil growled and hauled the Nightmare up by his shirtfront. Moose snarled and the man wilted in Neil's grip.

"Moose, you are the best dog," Aunt Judy declared.

Sky left them, moving painfully toward her horse waiting by the trees. The mist rose and flowed over them like stream of reflected moonlight. Silver and magical.

The stallion stamped one hoof and Sky put her arms around his neck, burying her face in his velvet coat and shining mane. His warmth spread through her, easing her hurts, soothing away her fears.

"Thank you," she whispered.

"*I waited a long time for you, Dear Heart,*" the unicorn whispered. "*It is good that you have come home again.*"

As the smoky mist enveloped the night, Sky stood with her hand curled into the horse's mane. The warmth of magic surged beneath her fingers and the unicorn spirit leaped upward, away from the white stallion. With a joyous toss of his head and a bugling call, the unicorn cantered away into the clouds.

Enthralled, Sky watched until her horse bunted her shoulder.

"Let's go get you a little sweet hay and a nice bed for the night," Sky murmured to him. He whickered affectionately and the two turned back toward the stable. The flames had subsided and the horsemen and women worked wearily to clear the debris and care for their horses.

The moonlight clearly showed Sky the path, and distantly, she could hear the echoes of the unicorn's hooves as he galloped in the mist.

Thank you for reading
The Nightmare and the Unicorn!

If you enjoyed this, please leave a review
on Amazon.com (even a sentence helps!)
so that other readers can more easily
find *The Nightmare and the Unicorn*.

You can find more exciting books by
Susan Brown at www.susanbrownwrites.com

And keep reading for excerpts from
other books by Susan Brown.

Enjoy!

And now a Sneak Peek at

Twelve
First Place Winner in Chanticleer's International Book Awards Competition

Another city, another run-down hotel. Jared longs for a normal life, but he is haunted by the Song that no one else hears and hunted for the twelve stones that guard humanity's essence. Jared and his twin Meghan are mercilessly stalked by the Titan, Kronos, risen from his prison to challenge the millennia of human dominance.

Frantic to save his family, Jared dares to learn the truth about his heritage. He wants to run, but the rocks show him what is at stake. Somehow, he will have to protect the twelve stones and defeat Kronos. Nothing else can save humanity.

You won't be able to put down this thrilling story weaving the world's mythology with a heart-pounding tale about what it means to be human.

Dragons of Frost and Fire

"I know she's still alive!"

A year ago her mother disappeared in an Alaskan blizzard, but Kit Soriano refuses to give up. Against all logic, propelled by recurring dreams of ice-white dragons and a magical silver knife, Kit journeys to the wilderness town of Silver Claw where her mother vanished. She's clearly not welcome, but her knife throbs with heat and her dreams show the impossible – mythical dragons are guarding her sleeping mother.

Desperate, Kit has no choice but to rely on Dai, who knows more than he says about the wild magic rippling beneath the surface of the town. She wants to trust him. But is he her friend or an enemy? If she's wrong, will she too be lost forever in the unforgiving Alaskan wilderness?

Twelve

by

Susan Brown

Bodhhgaya, India

Transformation

At first Deirdre grips the six-year-old twins' hands tightly, and at first Jared and Meghan are happy to press close. Jared twists to look back at the hotel sign, and stares at the letters: Hotel Bodhgaya Ashok. He doesn't know what the last two words are. He doesn't know where he is, except this place is called India. Most of the buildings have signs, but the words are written in the curly-cues and slants that his mother says is Indian writing.

Jared can't make it out.

This city makes him afraid, with its hot, hot air. Dust rises in the streets, so that when the wind blows he can see nothing but a reddish cloud. The crowded, smelly train had frightened him. Everyone shouted and laughed and talked in words he couldn't understand. The bus after that was worse – more crowded and smellier.

When Deirdre pauses for a moment, Jared shuts his eyes and tries again to imagine the place that is green and safe with a pattern of pink flowers on the floor. But with a jab of fear, he remembers that even in the dream, there are shadows lurking in cupboards and behind stone walls. He opens his eyes again and looks at his twin, but she is busy staring at everything.

Meghan isn't afraid at all. Ever. She loves this hot, strange place and is determined to meet all the people and try all the food sold from roadside tents. She tugs her hand loose, and before Deirdre can stop her, darts away, disappearing into the crowd.

"Oh, drat her!" Deirdre exclaims. She stands Jared by a tree. "Don't move. Not one step!"

She runs in search of her daughter.

Jared looks in every direction. Kronos, The Man Who Watches is staring at them again. Jared can feel it. His mother won't notice him while she chases Meghan.

There. At the edge of the streaming crowd...Jared sees the burning eyes in the pale face. Despite the still air, Kronos' black hair looks like it has been thrashed by a storm. Jared knows that no one else in the pushing crowd sees Kronos. If they did, their shadowed eyes would open wide with fear and their muttering voices would rise into screams. Kronos raises a hand to Jared, beckoning, commanding. Sunlight glimmers on his golden mark.

Jared squeezes his eyes shut, breathing hard, fighting the urge to follow the beckoning hand. His Mama told him to stay put.

"Jared!" Deirdre grabs his hand. He opens his eyes with relief. "At least one of you will stand still." She glares at Meghan who laughs and tosses her fire-red hair.

"The grandpa was nice." Meghan holds up a small orange that a toothless old man has given her.

Jared looks back to Kronos. He is gone now. With his mother and sister, Jared joins the mass of people walking down the road to the temple.

"This is the holiest place in India," Deirdre tells them. "The monks know things we don't understand. I hope..." She bites her lip. "I think they might help us..."

The temple rises like a pointed ant hill. Low walls of carved pinky-red rock direct the flow of the crowd. Most people swarm along a walkway. It looks like a parade with all the flowers and fluttering silk scarves. Deirdre pulls them forward, down stone steps and past another stream of people walking round and round the temple. Jared nearly falls over a man lying on his stomach with his arms stretched out.

"Is he hurt?" He clutches his mother's hand more tightly.

"No, he's praying." She steers them past more people lying on their stomachs and over to a wall, out of the press of people. "Shoes off, kids. We can't wear them in the temple."

His mom puts their shoes in her bag, and then in sock feet, they rejoin the crowd.

People pour through the gate and towards a huge open door. Jared, Meghan and Deirdre are swept along with them into a cool, dim room. Everyone sits on the floor.

An old man in baggy yellow clothes with a red shawl over one shoulder is speaking to the seated people. Deirdre leans forward, hands twisting in her lap. Jared's eyes fix on a huge gold statue of a seated man. Buddha. Many of the people are bowing to the statue. Meghan elbows her twin and points around the room. Every wall and even the ceiling are decorated with vast pictures. While the old man talks and talks, Jared stares open-mouthed at the paintings of scenery, people, gods and demons. Some are happy; some are crying; some are writhing their many arms and showing fangs.

One picture draws his eyes. It is The Man Who Watches, riding a horse breathing fire from its mouth and striking flames from its hooves. Jared hears the hoof beats, smells the acrid smoke...

"No!" he whispers. The sounds and smells fade. He thinks the smiling statue of Buddha may have chased Kronos away.

The old man at the front stops talking. Their mother surges up from the pillows and taking each of them by hand, approaches a yellow-robed monk.

"Excuse me," she says, "I have an appointment to see His Holiness Lama Choedak Jamyang." She drops the twins' hands to pull a letter from her bag. Her voice trembles. "I was told he can help me."

The monk nods. "He expects you. Also, his Holiness Lama Satya asks permission to visit with your children."

Deirdre looks at them doubtfully. "I don't know..."

"I'm not going," Meghan grips her mother's hand. "I want to come with you, Mama, and give our presents to the llama."

The monk looks calmly at Jared.

"I'll go," Jared says. Why did he say that?

The monk bows, hands pressed together. Another young monk appears at his side. Deirdre and Meghan go with him. Nervously, Jared follows the older one along narrow corridors filled with weird smells and quiet footsteps.

"It is custom to bow three times when entering the presence of His Holiness," the monk whispers and opens a door. Jared steps into a room ablaze with color. Red walls are highlighted by yellow cloth that hangs like curtains or drapes across the furniture. A soccer ball lies under a table. On a raised platform, a boy about ten, sits cross-legged. He is dressed like the monks.

Jared stares, then says, "Hi." Behind him, the monk is bowing.

The boy smiles. "Hi, Jared," he replies. "Didn't Meghan come?"

Jared shakes his head. "She's with my mother."

The boy's expression becomes serious again and he jumps down from the platform. "I am sorry she is not here. I have something important to show you."

He heads out of the room and down the hallway. Not knowing what else to do, Jared follows. They walk down several more narrow corridors, all scented like smoky flowers, then come into the sunlight in an open courtyard. A large twisted tree grows in the center. Bits of gold glimmer on its trunk. Masses of flowers are strewn on the ground and white scarves tied to the branches lift and fall in the breeze.

Jared thinks the place should be full of people, but he and the boy are alone.

"It is under the ancestor of this fig tree that Buddha received enlightenment," the boy says. "And here," he leads Jared to a slab of brick-red stone, "is the stone on which he sat. It is the only stone strong enough to have held the world together when the transformation came. It is the center of the universe."

As though he had been told to do it, Jared steps forward and stands on the stone. Heat gathers in a pool, rises through his feet and floats up into his body, lifting him into the air.

"I'm flying!" he cries. "Can Meghan come and do this?"

The boy shakes his head. "There is only this one moment when the flow of time has stilled and she did not come. You alone are chosen."

Jared flaps his arms trying to rise higher.

The boy takes something from inside his robe – a stone, the same reddish color as the one Jared hovers over. He offers it. "I have guarded this for you through all my lifetimes. It is carved with the eyes of Buddha and holds the key to transformation and enlightenment."

"What's that?" Jared's hands close on the rock and his mind glows.

"The ancient gods cannot change. They are what they are. Neither love nor death nor suffering can transform their hearts and spirits. Only humans can become more than they were. One day people may become greater than the gods. They fear this."

"Jared!" Deirdre's voice pierces the air. Startled, Jared's feet touch the ground and he jumps off the stone. Like ghosts melting back into reality, people and chatter fill the courtyard. The stone is now covered in bright cloth, with oranges, money, and bowls of rice heaped over it. The boy smiles, then walks back into the temple.

Deirdre and Meghan run to Jared. "Thank goodness!" Deirdre hugs him. "None of the other monks spoke English. I thought I'd lost you."

"There wasn't a llama," Meghan complains as they put their shoes back on. "Just an old man with glasses. Did you see a llama?"

Jared shakes his head. "Just a boy. He gave me a stone."

For the first time Jared really looks at it. The eyes of Buddha look back. More of the curly writing he can't read has been carved into the stone.

"The old man gave me a handkerchief." Meghan displays a small square of white silk with a faded picture and the same curly writing.

"Well, at least you two got something out of this trip." Deirdre takes their hands and hauls them toward the gate. "Come on kids, we have hurry. If we're lucky, we can still make it to New York by next Friday. Pat has an audition set up for me."

"I thought we were staying," Jared protests.

"No," Deirdre says. "The Lama says he can't protect me from my demons. We have to keep going."

256   Susan Brown

Part I

Seattle, Washington

Chapter 1

The Song

March rain splattered down, cold and insistent, as fifteen-year-old Jared stepped off the San Francisco to Seattle bus and looked around. Another city, another bus station. He hefted his backpack onto his shoulders and took a couple of quick steps to catch up to his mom and Meghan. It had seemed like a miracle when this job came through – they'd been down to their last hundred dollars. If the job worked out, if they didn't have to run, the family might get a few dollars into a savings account again.

If they didn't have to run. Head down, eyelids slightly lowered, Jared scanned the milling crowds. A grandmother here, a homeless man there, a few kids running wild while their harassed parents groped through bags. Nothing to set the short hairs on his neck prickling. No hint of the hunters who never gave up, never seemed to rest.

Meghan and his mom had paused in front of a snack bar, Meghan clearly arguing to immediately make up for their missed lunch; his mom just as clearly urging for her to wait, to conserve their few remaining dollars. Jared swept his eyes over the crowd again. Everything ordinary. He let out his pent-up breath and eased through the jostling crowd of travelers.

And then...*the Song*. Jared stopped cold. He could feel sweat forming on his forehead and upper lip. He could hear it – the singing had started again.

He lifted his head like a dog to a scent. The singing was clear, very clear. This time... surely this time, he would be able to make out the words. Jared shook his head, tried to separate the unearthly melody from noises surrounding him – the growl of traffic, shouting passengers, and drumming rain. But there was too much confusion.

Over there...the singing came from the end of the station. He ran through the crowd, dodging bags, boxes and people. At an empty loading platform, he stopped and shut his eyes tightly. This time he would arrow himself to the source of the singing – finally hear all the words.

A picture crowded into his mind. He could hear everything in the bus terminal, but behind it, like a brightening movie screen, the thrumming began...

Noise of a heart beating too fast...beating in terror....
Fist clutching....
Behind...red eyes...the red-eared dogs of night...
howling...closer...closer....hunting through the woods...
baying for blood...
Heart throbbing...
But the last Guardian will follow the lines of power
and sing the Song of Light...He begins the chanting
melody...it lifts into the wind.
Jared can hear it now...it fills him again...he can
sing with the old man...

A hard hand tugged his sleeve. "Hey kid, spare some change?"

The Song shattered. Jared blinked, confused. A raggedy teenager, only a couple of years older than himself, held out her hand. Her eyes were grey nuggets in a white face.

"What?"

"Change," the girl whined. "I got nowhere to sleep. Nothing to eat...you got some money? Something in your pack to help me out?"

Her hand inserted itself under the flap, fingers searching.

"No way," Jared twisted away. "Hey! What do you think you're doing?"

"I could trade," the girl whispered. "I got this to trade…"

She held up her fist, so close to Jared's face that he could scarcely make out the twisted shape of a tattoo above the knuckle of her middle finger. It seemed to be a distorted spider…shimmering in front of his eyes.

"Hey! Get away!" the girl shrieked.

A black and white dog pushed between Jared and the girl, growling deep in its throat. The girl faltered back, made shooing motions with her hands, then with a hoarse sob turned and ran. The dog's growling stopped, his head raised and with an air of all business taken care of, scratched his ear with a hind foot. Without a glance at Jared, he turned and trotted through the crowds.

"Now, that was weird," Jared muttered. Almost as weird, he thought, as trying to learn a Song that no one else could hear. Or as weird as carrying ten heavy rocks in his backpack and one more stone in his pocket as his family gypsied around the world. The Song was silent again. Slowly, he wove back through the thinning crowd to his mom and sister.

"Jared," his mom's voice rose over the hubbub. "Get the bags, hon."

His small family had not paid any attention to his dash through the crowd. Jared wasn't really surprised – he had long since become aware that the Song sometimes suppressed time, or memory, or just plain noticing. With a nod to his mom, he picked up two suitcases; Meghan dropped the bag she'd held to push back her long red hair with both hands.

"The rain's turning me into a frizzball." She pulled an elastic from her pocket and caught her hair into a fat ponytail. Like her brother, she carried a bulging, frayed backpack over her shoulders. Hers was weighted down with books, music and a flute; Jared's shoulders ached with the weight of his fist-sized rocks.

"Now, if you just turn left, Mrs. Singer," the ticket agent was telling their mother, "and go along Stewart about two blocks, there's the Regency Inn right there." He beamed at her. "It's a nice place. Better than that Carmen Hotel you were talking about."

"Thank you, so much." Deirdre smiled charmingly and turned back to her children.

"Another guy?" Meghan teased softly. She hoisted her bag higher on her shoulders.

"Oh, don't be silly," her mom shushed her. "He's just a nice person trying to be helpful." She picked up her own suitcase and led them toward the street.

Outside the station, an old man with a curling white beard sat with a sign:

Real Change, Seattle's Homeless Newspaper.
Help the Homeless Help Themselves.

Jared eyed at the man's tattered clothes and turned his head away. His stomach knotted. Homeless came after broke. His family was awfully close to broke....

Meghan's gaze slid past the dirt and rips, up to the man's face. She smiled. "Wet today," she said.

His clear eyes sparkled. "Not so bad as yesterday. It'll come onto sun in a bit. Have a good afternoon."

"Thank you," she called back.

"Why'd you talk to him?" Jared hissed.

"Why didn't you?" she retorted. "He's broke. That's hard enough without being invisible, too."

Jared flushed and glanced back. The black and white dog stood with its front paws propped on the old man's knees. His master was talking to him and gently rubbing his ears.

The family trudged down Stewart Street, giving the Regency Inn only a brief look of regret. The Seattle Space Needle, built for the '62 World's Fair, towered in the distance.

Above, city crows wheeled and squawked. At Sixth Avenue they turned left, away from the Space Needle, and kept on walking. Expensive shops gave way to shabby stores. To his right, down a steep hill, Jared could see the rippling glint of Puget Sound.

"How far is it?" Meghan grunted.

"Another couple of blocks. It's very central – close to Pike Place Market and the historic part of town," Deirdre Singer said.

Jared and Meghan exchanged depressed glances. Historic always meant old and run-down when it came to their rooms.

Rain fell more heavily. Jared's dark hair slicked down and hung in his eyes. Despite the ponytail, Meghan's writhed into tight corkscrews. Finally, they cut through a parking lot to a grey hotel crouched behind an office building.

"Sweet," Meghan muttered.

The door squealed. Light barely penetrated the lobby. Behind the counter, a young man put down his phone, and stood to greet them with a wide smile.

Jared dropped the bags. An air of mildew and dust drifted upward from the threadbare carpet. An ancient elevator clanked open. No one got out.

"Ghosts," Meghan whispered.

Their mom headed to the desk.

"Welcome to The Carmen," the clerk said. "Marquis is my name, and I'm here to make your stay as comfortable as your favorite dream. Your name, please, Ma'am?"

"Deirdre Singer. My children and I have a reservation."

Marquis typed something into a computer.

"Yes, Ma'am, here it is." Marquis smiled widely again. "Six weeks. That's a long time to be sightseeing."

"I'll be working. I have a role in *The Phantom of the Opera* revival."

"No way!" Marquis exclaimed. "I thought they all was staying at the Warwick."

"The main players are. I have a small part a friend arranged for me."

"You sing then?"

"Whenever I can."

"Well, well!" Marquis rubbed his hands together. "A star staying at our hotel. I'll give you the best efficiency suite in the house. Big and at the back. None of that traffic noise. Fully equipped with a range top, fridge and dishes. And no extra charge!"

"Thank you." Mrs. Singer smiled. "We appreciate it."

"Yes, Ma'am. Comfortable as a dream. Take the elevator to sixth floor then turn right.

Corner room on your left."

The twins picked up the bags and followed their mom into the elevator.

"I think this dream's going to be a nightmare," Meghan said. The doors crashed shut, opened a couple of inches, and then banged shut again.

"At least there's a nice desk clerk," Mrs. Singer pointed out. "That makes it more pleasant."

"And the hotel's in a business area," Jared added. "We can go sightseeing without getting mugged."

Over the last few years, the hotels had gotten worse and worse as their mom struggled harder and harder for bit parts in the operas and traveling musical productions that supported them. Most big cities had their own opera companies and regular theater players. Deirdre picked up the leavings – this time taking a part in the chorus. The contracted actor had broken her leg.

That was the way it always was now. Sometimes a singer would get sick, or take time off for a baby, or quarrel with the director. The production company would frantically call the agents, and Pat, their mom's agent would call Deirdre, telling her what city she had to get to – right away.

"I fill in for disaster," Deirdre had said wryly. The elevator clanged to a stop. The doors squealed open.

A young man, unshaven with greasy hair, eyed them from the hall.

"Up or down?" he demanded.

"Up," Deirdre said.

He grunted. Deirdre pushed the "Close Door" button. Nothing happened. They stared at the man in the hall and he stared at them. His eyes slid over to Meghan and his expression changed. Jared stepped in front of his sister. She elbowed him.

"What floor..." Deirdre began to ask. The doors clanged shut.

"I know I'm going to just love this place," Meghan said.

"Only six weeks, sweetie. Seattle's a great city. When the weather clears we can rent a car and drive to the ocean beaches. They're spectacular."

A sudden memory of sound...pounding waves...pounding footsteps. Jared stiffened. The call was from a place by the ocean. But, how could his whole family have been maneuvered here from hundreds of miles away? Did the magic in the rocks completely control their lives?

Automatically, Jared closed his fingers around the rock in his pocket...remembering.

DRAGONS OF
FROST AND FIRE

DRAGONS OF EARTH,
WATER, FIRE AND AIR

BY

SUSAN BROWN

ONE

The floatplane touched down on Silver Lake, spewing sheets of water into the air. Pressing her icy hands against the passenger window, Kit Soriano tried to force back a shudder. This far north, the Rocky Mountains peaks thrust into the sky like teeth – old teeth, cruel teeth, with glacial lips pulled back into a snarl.

"Silver Claw," the pilot called over his shoulder. "Last stop of humanity."

David Soriano peered out his own window, then reached his hand across the seat to grip his daughter's cold fingers. Silently they stared at this terrible place where they had come to find answers. Beyond the narrow beach, a few weather-beaten buildings made up the town. Past that, mountainous ice caps blended into clouds in every direction. At the north end of the lake, a glacier hundreds of feet high lay between the mountains like a mythic sleeping monster. Aqua and blue ice shone translucent in the sunlight.

"This is what mom tried to describe...." Kit gripped the dragon-shaped knife hidden in her pocket – she was going to need every ounce of magic her mother had said it possessed. There was nothing else left for her to believe in.

The pilot eased the plane to the dock and cut the engine. Kit's ears still thrummed with the vibrations, when a series of rumbles and cracks rolled across the lake and through the skin of the plane. An ice monolith slowly split from the glacier and crashed into the water. Spray shot a hundred feet into the air. Shock waves raced across the lake, rocking the plane.

When Kit gasped and clutched the armrests, the pilot laughed. "That's Silver Snake Glacier." He pointed to the ice cliff. "In spring it breaks up some – calving, it's called. But you've never heard anything like the roars and howls that come from that ice snake in winter. I was holed up here one year when an early blizzard rolled in. I swear I thought the noise alone would kill me."

Kit forced herself to stare impassively at the forbidding Alaskan landscape. "I'm not afraid of noise." She would not, would not let this place defeat her.

The pilot shrugged. "Hope you're not planning to stay too long," he warned. "Once winter gets her talons into this country, it can cost you your life to go outside of town."

"We'll be back in New York by winter," her father said. "We're only staying a couple of weeks."

Until we find her, Kit vowed.

The pilot heaved himself out of his chair, wrestled with the door, and showed them how to scramble down to the pontoon and then jump onto the dock. Kit shivered. Even though it was mid-August, the Alaskan air was cold through her fleece vest. She warmed up a little as they unloaded their gear.

A dozen of the town's residents drifted down to the dock, but Kit kept her eyes off the kids. Those kids had lured her mother to Silver Claw – nearly a quarter of them were albino, a genetic mutation. Dr. Nora Reits had been a genetics researcher. Nearly a year ago, she had disappeared without a trace in an early fall storm in Silver Claw.

Kit again touched the silver pocketknife nestled in her pocket. Magic find her, she prayed silently. Warmth tingled against her skin – the connection was still strong. Relieved, Kit turned her energy to separating their gear from the supplies ordered by the residents.

A lot of folks were on the dock now. In spite of herself, Kit sneaked a look under her lashes. The albino kids had snow-white hair and glacier blue eyes. Unlike some albino people, their sparkling glances showed good eyesight and they glowed with health.

"Dr. Soriano?" A big man with red hair stuck out his hand to Kit's father. "I'm Pat Kelly, mayor of this place. I wish I could welcome you here under better circumstances."

Dr. Soriano shook hands with the mayor. "We appreciate your willingness to let us get some closure on my wife's disappearance."

The mayor nodded. "I understand your feelings. We lost one of our own boys in that blizzard. This is a hard land – beautiful, but hard."

"Yes," Dr. Soriano said gazing at the ring of jagged peaks. "But I'm hoping the clinic will be a useful return for your hospitality."

"My mother-in-law will keep you busy, even if no one else does," Pat replied with an easy smile. "It's a long flight to Anchorage when the problems are the aches and pains old folks feel every time the weather changes."

As Kit reached up to grab the rest of their bags, she drew a deep breath. After all the setbacks and problems, she could hardly believe they were really here.

It had taken her father weeks to work out their journey. Getting to Silver Claw would be no problem – a regular flight from New York City to Anchorage and then they could book seats on the floatplane that delivered supplies to the town every couple of weeks. But inquiries about where to stay had been discouraging. There was apparently no reliable Internet connection that far north, and so all communication was by snail mail. A letter from the town council, signed Mary McGough, Secretary, had been brusque. The council regretted there was no hotel in Silver Claw.

Dr. Soriano's lips had thinned as he read the letter aloud to Kit.

"Isn't she the person Mom rented a room and office from? Wasn't it above a store or something?" Kit had asked.

"Yup," her dad said. "Let's try this one more time." That evening, he wrote back politely requesting that he and his daughter rent the room that his wife had previously occupied.

Three weeks later a second response from the town secretary stated that she was using the space Dr. Reits had rented for storage and so it was no longer available.

"I don't think they want us," Dr. Soriano had told his daughter over macaroni and cheese.

"I don't care. You promised me..." Kit looked challengingly into his eyes.

"And I keep my promises," he'd said. "Have some salad. It's only a little brown."

After dinner, while Kit had loaded the dishwasher and then tackled physics homework, he had written a third letter to the town council.

Dear Members of the Council,

I am hoping that we will still be able to work out the details of my daughter's and my visit. We are coming to Silver Claw. As east coast city people, we don't have a lot of experience with wilderness camping, but we will come with tents and backpacks and set up on the glacier itself, if necessary.

However, I have a proposal for you. I am a medical doctor and I'm willing to operate a free clinic for the residents of the area in return for accommodation and supplies while my daughter and I are in town.

We will be arriving on August 12th, with or without a place to stay.

Sincerely,
David Soriano, M.D.

The next response came from Pat Kelly instead of the secretary and it was a lot friendlier. A new cabin had been built for his family and he was willing to let Kit and her dad use it for a couple of weeks. He sympathized with the Soriano's need to see the town where Dr. Reits had spent her last few weeks. The residents of the town would be pleased to welcome them.

Kit and her dad flew from New York on August 11th, spent the night in Anchorage and the next morning boarded the small floatplane.

After all her thinking and worrying, it seemed to Kit that she was in a dream as she stood at the edge of the dock and gazed across the wild landscape. The glacier glinted, shifting colors like a living, crystal animal.

Mayor Kelly turned from Dr. Soriano to the people standing on the dock behind him. "Here, you kids give a hand. Kirsi...Dai...grab some of the bags."

Two of the older albino teenagers, a girl and boy, left the group. Both were tall and strong, their white-blonde hair ruffling in the steady breeze. They radiated health and were incredibly good looking. Mesmerized, Kit realized with a small shock that they were better than good looking – they were the most beautiful teens she had ever seen. They were graceful, perfectly proportioned, and there wasn't even a zit to be seen. Kit thought she could hate them just for that.

As Kirsi leaned down to pick up luggage, she turned cold blue eyes toward Kit. "You shouldn't have come here," she hissed. "You soft city people don't belong." She hoisted the heavy pack over her shoulder with ease and strode away without a backward glance.

The breeze off the lake quickened. Kit shivered.

"You'll get used to the temperatures," Dai said beside her. He appeared about seventeen, a year older than she was. Up close, Kit thought his looks alone could warm her up.

Kit made a grab for her peace of mind and shrugged. "I'm not afraid of the cold."

"That's good because sometimes we get a lot of it. I'm Dai Phillips." He stuck out his hand to shake.

Kit hesitated a split second, then shook his hand. It was so very warm and firm. A responding flash of heat shot through her. This was not normal for her at all.

"I'm Kit." At home the kids either didn't touch or did hand slaps and fist bumps. Nobody under forty shook hands.

Patrick Kelly picked up one of Dr. Soriano's medical cases. "We do appreciate your willingness to run a health clinic even for two weeks, Doc," he said. "Hey there, Jancy. You, Mikey. Help the doctor with his bags." Two red-haired children each picked up a suitcase. "Dai, are you going to stand around all day or are you going to help that little girl out?"

Hot color flushed Dai's face. "Yes, Uncle Pat," he said under his breath. He reached for a duffel. "This yours, Kit?"

"I'll get it," she said. "I packed it. I can carry it." She hoisted it up and over her thin shoulder. "And I'm sixteen...not a little girl." She knew she looked too young and fragile to be in the wilderness. But she also knew that her slender bones were connected to tough muscle.

"Okay," Dai said. "But it's a bit of a hike to the cabin and I'm used to the path."

"Whatever." Kit slid the bag back to the dock, refusing to allow even a flicker of relief to cross her face. She'd jammed it with everything she thought might be useful – survival gear, guidebooks, contour maps, compass, and a Swiss Army knife.

Dai's deep blue eyes searched her own.

"What?" Kit demanded. His intense gaze unnerved her.

Dai leaned over and lifted the bag like it weighed six ounces instead of sixty pounds. "It's good you've come to us – you're the kind that's called."

"Called? Called what?"

"Called by the mountains and wilderness. By the heart that beats up there." Again, his eyes pierced her own. "Your mother was the same. You both belong here. I feel it."

Kit felt a lump rise sharply in her throat so she turned away and stared at the town as though fascinated by the worn clapboard structures. Kirsi stood at the top of the path, arms folded, looking stonily down at the people on the dock. Kit stared back defiantly.

"My mother didn't belong here and I don't either," she turned and told Dai. "I'm going to find out what happened to her and then you'll never see me again."

She picked up a bag and marched up the path toward Kirsi. Other men and children took the rest of the luggage. The remainder of the people finished unloading boxes of supplies from the plane and began hauling them up the hill toward town. Dai strode after her, whistling off-key. Kit glanced back at him. She had never seen anyone so vibrantly alive. And he had talked about her mother. Had he gotten to know her? Would he have information that would lead Kit to her?

Abruptly she slowed down, matching her steps to his. But with a cool glance, he trudged faster away from her, still whistling. Kit's eyes narrowed, but she followed without comment. In a moment she had reached Kirsi. The girl looked her over like she was a dead fish washed onto the shore.

"Stay away from Dai. He has no use for your kind," Kirsi mocked.

"What kind is that, Kirsi?" Kit demanded.

The girl's lips curled into a sneer. "A weak outlander. You'll be very sorry you ever came here." She shoved past Kit, knocking her off balance.

Regaining her footing, Kit glared after her. "I think you will be surprised." She made no effort to catch up, waiting instead for her dad and the others.

"The house is this way, Doctor." Mayor Kelly gestured along an overgrown dirt road that edged the lake. "The clinic building is in town, but this cabin has an incredible view of Silver Snake."

The cabin sat on a rounded hill overlooking the lake. The building was made of shaped logs, with a fresh look about them. Shuttered windows along the sides were wide and evenly spaced. A long porch was angled to face the glacier.

Everyone trooped through the screen door, but Kit dropped her bag and leaned on the railing, looking towards mountains and ice. Behind her, voices filled the cabin. But out here, the stillness folded into a sense of being on the edge of another world. Kit breathed deeply, tasting the tang of wilderness, and another acrid scent – sweet and bitter mingled. She tossed her head to let the clean air wash over her. After the long despair, she was coming alive again. Kit remembered how her mother had described this place in her letters....

Silver Snake Glacier drapes the mountains like a huge sleeping animal. It really seems alive, shifting with every color that ever existed. I hope you get to see it some day – it must be one of the wonders of the world! I am going to hike up there and see if I can fathom its secrets. Something that otherworldly must have secrets, Kit. Devin tells me the glacier is riddled with crevasses and caves – a beautiful but deadly creature, I guess. It wakes when the winter storms howl over the mountains....

Dai came out on the porch and stood beside her. Despite herself, Kit was too aware of the warmth he radiated. Of those broad shoulders and lithe build. She'd never been this aware of the boys at home. Pheromones. He must be radiating mutated pheromones and she was feeling every one of them.

Another crack shattered the quiet of the town.

"Loud, isn't it?" Kit said turning to him. She froze. His eyes were a deeper blue. She'd swear they had darkened. Ridiculous. Even weird eyes, genetically mutated eyes, shouldn't change color. It had to be a trick of the light.

"This is a great time of year to be in Silver Claw." Dai's expression once again lightened to an easy smile. "There's hiking, hunting and fishing during the day and bonfires and get-togethers at night. Mary McGough at the general store gets in movies now and then."

"Sounds terrific," Kit said, "But I already have plans." She forced herself to turn away from those hot, mesmerizing eyes and look back at the cold waters of the lake. Her mother had said native legends put some kind of mythic beast in those cold depths.

Then Dai's hand, hot and strong, gripped her arm. "There are no other plans in Silver Claw," Dai told her. "You'll be smart to listen to me." The warning in his voice was unmistakable.

"Or what?" Kit challenged. How friendly or how dangerous was this guy? He was like fire and ice. Already this place was freaking her out, all beauty and danger.

His eyes shifted even darker, making that weird sense of warmth flare through her again. She didn't know whether he would have answered or not because they were interrupted by the door swinging open. The moment bled away.

"Kit," her dad called. "Which bedroom do you want?"

"Excuse me," Kit stepped past Dai and followed her father.

Inside, several men and women had settled on the sofas and chairs. Dai came in after her and crossed over to Kirsi who leaned against the far wall. As they stood talking in quiet voices and sometimes glancing in her direction, Kit felt another surge of anger. Were they talking about her? And why should she care?

In the meantime, two women were opening and shutting the cupboard doors in the kitchen area, calling on Dr. Soriano to admire how thoroughly they had stocked up for him.

"My wife is bringing some lasagna over," the mayor said. "A bit of a welcome to let you get yourself unpacked and settled tonight."

"Dr. Soriano," Dai struck in, "my mother said I'm to ask you for dinner tomorrow at seven, if you don't have other plans.... " He glanced mockingly at Kit.

"Great," Dr. Soriano said. "That's very kind. We'll be there. Now Kit, what about that bedroom?"

Three bedrooms opened off the kitchen-dining-living area, so Kit chose one where the window faced the glacier. While her dad chatted with the people who had helped bring their belongings up, Kit hauled in her bags. Methodically, she unpacked her clothing and filled the drawers of the wooden dresser. She left all her survival gear in the duffel bag, zipped it up, and pushed it far under the bed.

"Kit!" her dad called. "The most marvelous dinner is being spread out here for us!"

The main room was packed with big, loud strangers. It seemed like everyone who had come down to the dock had migrated up to the cabin and brought a few friends along. Did any of those open, friendly faces hide the secret of her mother's disappearance? She wanted to shout at them, demand they tell her what they knew, but instead she forced herself to paste on a fake smile.

"Please, you must stay," her father was urging.

With only a brief show of reluctance, everyone dug into the lasagna, salad, bread and meat that all seemed to have magically appeared. Kit picked among the dishes and settled in the remotest corner of the sofa. Dai left Kirsi and perched on the arm beside her.

Ignoring him, Kit took a bite of the dark meat. Flavor exploded in her senses.

"Backstrap," Dai said. "The tenderest and tastiest part of a moose."

Kit put her fork down but chewed on. It was good – different from anything else she'd tasted. "Great!" she mumbled through her full mouth.

"You're honored," Dai said. "That's probably the last of Uncle Pat's winter store. He's the best hunter in town, but we try to only hunt moose in the fall and winter."

Kit cut another piece of meat and popped it in her mouth. "The only moose I ever saw for real was in a zoo. It was big and sad looking so it seems cruel to hunt them."

"We have to eat and there aren't many fast food restaurants in the wilderness," Dai replied. "Besides, those hamburgers don't come from carrots."

Kit took a big bite of her bread to avoid answering. She knew he was right, but she didn't want to acknowledge that the rules were different here in Silver Claw. With mountains, lakes and glaciers surrounding them, they hunted to eat. They killed to survive.

A burst of laughter filled the cabin. She tried another bite of backstrap. It tasted fine on her tongue. Kit looked around at all the handsome, strong faces. She would learn what they knew, she vowed. And if they had secrets, she would find them.

Despite their protests about letting the Sorianos unpack, the townspeople didn't leave for hours. By the time Kit could finally get to bed, she was too wound up to sleep.

Outside, twilight had eased over the land, casting the mountains into dark relief. The luminous hands on her watch read 11:03 but the sky still shone dusky blue. Kit sat on her bed, wrapped in a quilt, looking out toward Silver Snake Glacier.

It drew her, called her, just as Dai had said it would. Her mom's letters had described the hours she spent hiking by the glacier. She'd written that the sight and sound of the ancient ice relieved her frustrations when the townspeople refused to cooperate with her research.

And that's how I'll start, Kit decided; she would go to the places her mother had described, try to find some kind of clue her mother may have left behind. Looking out the open window at the immense distances and peaks, Kit wondered with a sinking heart whether she would be able to find the places from the descriptions in the letters. In New York, hemmed in by buildings and streetlights, she had not been able to grasp the vastness of the landscape.

Her father came in, set a lantern on the table beside her bed and sat down.

"They seem like nice people around here," he said at last.

Kit rolled her eyes. "That's what Mom said...until they found out what she was doing."

Her hand slipped under her pillow to touch the knife and the packet of letters. In the last one, Nora Reits had written in an excited scrawl from her office over the general store. She had said she would try to slip the letter into the outgoing mail sack before the floatplane arrived. This flight, she was sure, would bring lab results for the blood samples she had coaxed from one albino boy. Kit got the letter two days after her mother disappeared.

"Kit, it was a simple hiking accident," her dad said. "You know she hiked up there alone, even though the weather was threatening."

"Then why did the lab results disappear?" Kit demanded. "And the searchers didn't find a body. They're keeping her somewhere. I know it! My knife...."

"Kit, don't start about that knife again." Her father rubbed his hand over his face; his eyes were exhausted. Kit fell silent.

If only he would believe what Kit knew against all reason was true. Her mother was alive.

Another crack reverberated through the air. The lantern flickered. Somewhere, out there, Kit knew her mother was alive.

About Award-Winning Author, Susan Brown

What if? What if the extraordinary erupts into an ordinary life? Adventure, mystery, and magic fuel Susan Brown's imagination and writing, propelling her towards more and more stories for book-lovers who also live in wonder.

Susan lives with her border collie rescue dogs amid wild woods and overgrown gardens in Snohomish, Washington. From there she supervises her three daughters, assorted sons-in-law and two grandsons. It's a great way to be a writer!

Find more information, free stories, and news about upcoming books at:
http://www.susanbrownwrites.com

Susan Brown is also a founding member of the Writers Cooperative of the Pacific Northwest.
http://www.writers-coop.com

Made in the USA
Middletown, DE
28 April 2021